IT'S ABOUT
ABILITY
(NOT DISABILITY)

IT'S ABOUT ABILITY (NOT DISABILITY)

AARON PHILIP
WITH TONYA BOLDEN

BALZER + BRAY

An Imprint of HarperCollins*Publishers*

Balzer + Bray is an imprint of HarperCollins Publishers.

This Kid Can Fly: It's About Ability (NOT Disability)
Text copyright © 2016 by Tonya Bolden
Illustrations pages 155, 169, and 173 copyright © by Aaron Philip
Photos pages 11, 12, 29, 36, 37, 38, 41, 47, 75, 85, 115, and 167
courtesy of Aaron Philip
Photo page 102 copyright © by Alan Govenar

Library of Congress Control Number: 2015950987
ISBN 978-0-06-240354-4

Typography by Jenna Stempel
16 17 18 19 20 CG/RRDH 10 9 8 7 6 5 4 3 2 1

First Edition

I dedicate this book to everyone with and with-
out a disability who wants to step up, be bold
and creative, and make change in the world.
—A.P.

INTRO

So you're probably wondering: Who is this kid writing his memoir?

Aren't only old people supposed to do this? Or maybe you read the title and thought: Aha! This kid invented a jet pack and now I'll learn his secrets! Nope, sorry. Although, I wish! (Maybe that'll be my next book.)

As for this book, one of the reasons I wrote it is because I'm a kid with CP and I get around in a wheel-chair. Think about it: When was the last time you saw somebody, young or old, in a wheelchair? On the street? In a store? In your school? How many people do you know who practically live in wheelchairs? If you're like most people, you're probably scratching your head and thinking, er, um . . .

And I'm here to help you with that. If you keep reading this book you'll get to know a lot about me, then you'll be able to say—yeah! I do know at least one guy in a chair. Plus, I'm betting that you'll discover that while our lives might be superdifferent in some ways, we have a lot in common, too. . . .

Thanks for reading.

Welcome to Aaronland.

1
ROAR!

"Aaron, it's OK to be yourself!"

That was a huge moment for me—a real news flash in my brain as I rolled out of an office building in Lower Manhattan. Up on its tenth floor, in a humongous open space, I had given a talk about my life, my hopes, my dreams. I had welcomed close to two hundred people into Aaronland.

The date was October 29, 2013. Twelve-year-old me had just rocked it at Tumblr!

This was not my first time at Tumblr's HQ. A couple of months earlier I had the incredible honor of having a one on one with Tumblr's creator, the awesome David Karp.

I couldn't believe that this rich and famous and brilliant man could have any interest in *me*. I wasn't rich. I wasn't famous. True, I had some skills as an illustrator but I was a long way from brilliant. Yet, to my utter amazement, when David Karp met with me in June 2013 he seemed genuinely interested in me and my Tumblr blog. I think he was touched to see how I was using his creation. Near the end of our meeting in his really cool office, it was like something out of a movie: Karp invited me back—this time to speak to his *entire* staff.

Saying yes was easy, but as the date got closer and closer the more insanely nervous I became. It wasn't the first time I had addressed a group of grown-ups. But this was so different.

The audience was gonna be way bigger, I knew. Plus, I idolized David Karp. I worried about messing up, letting him down. Even scarier, I knew I'd be videotaped because Natalie Morales from the *Today* show was going to be there. What if I bombed in front of her, in front of David Karp, in front of his coders and designers and engineers—in front of the entire universe? I was *so* nervous.

So nervous—even though I prepared my presentation and practically memorized it.

So nervous—even though I role-played with Deb Fisher, one of my occupational therapists.

On that October day, instead of being in school, I was on my way to Tumblr's HQ, and I was a wreck, feeling so unsure of myself. Then came the moment when I rolled up to the front of that humongous room. Ten thousand maniac butterflies invaded my stomach. As David Karp introduced me, those butterflies partied hard. Then, in five, four, three, two—

I wasn't long into my presentation when those butterflies went on their way.

I forgot about the cameras.

I forgot about how big the audience was.

I forgot that I was addressing some of the most creative and innovative people on the planet.

I simply had my say. Let myself be myself. I even went off script a couple of times.

After my presentation and a Q&A—the fastest thirty-something minutes of my life—I was overwhelmed by the applause. It felt so amazing to have all those eyes on me. I felt amazing. I also felt—

Creative.

Ecstatic.

Shocked.

Lucky.

Proud.

Most of all, I felt validated. Nobody was looking past me. Nobody was looking through me. Nobody was trying to avoid eye contact with me or making me feel like I made them uncomfortable, like I was some alien being.

My presentation included a short video about snippets of my life. For the soundtrack I had picked Katy Perry's "Roar" because it's about the way I want to feel when I'm in school, when I'm out on the street, when I'm making art, when I'm dreaming.

When I rocked it at Tumblr I felt like I had roared. Like I was a fighter. Like I was a champion. Like I could continue to roar—even fly!—despite the challenges I face all the time.

2
PREEMIE ME

I weighed only two-and-a-half pounds when I arrived on the scene two months early in a place radically different from where I live now: gritty New York City.

I was born in a place a lot more laid-back, and cool in its own way. There are mango, calabash, and tamarind trees, and wild animals like fallow deer, loggerhead turtles, lizards, bats, and racer snakes. Barracudas lurk in turquoise water so clear and perfect it almost looks fake. During the day you might see pelicans, egrets, and ospreys. At night you can hear the mad music of tree frogs and cicadas. It's a place with 365 peachy-pink-sand beaches—"one for each day of the year," as the saying goes. (Don't ask about leap year.)

If you've guessed that I was born in the Caribbean— you guessed right! On March 15, 2001, I, Aaron Rorie Petrone Philip, was born in St. John's, the capital of Antigua and Barbuda.

My first bed was an incubator because of my under-developed lungs. Mom, very sick herself, was at the hospital all day every day, rooting for me. Dad checked in on me once or twice during the day, then returned and stayed in the evenings until the hospital made him and Mom go home.

After two months of that, I was finally strong enough for my parents, Petrone and Lydia Philip, to take me, their one and only, home. There, they'd have to cut newborn Pampers in half just to fit me. That's how tiny I was.

Home was about twenty miles southeast of St. John's, in the fishing village of Seatons, where Mom and Dad grew up. Our beautiful home sat on nearly a half acre of land that had a bunch of trees, like palm, lemon, lime, pomegranate, and soursop with its prickly green fruit. Besides the fruit trees, we always had a big bounty from Mom's garden. During the rainy season (September–November) our huge backyard was a veggie wonderland—Mom grew everything from cucumbers and corn to pumpkin and antrobers (aka eggplant).

Though I didn't have a strong start, my parents kept believing that I'd catch up and become a robust baby boy, but I didn't. The fact that something was wrong with me really hit home one evening in November 2001. Returning from the babysitter, Mom and Dad held my hands, coaxing me to walk up the front steps. Instead of cooperating, I kept my left leg hovering above the ground. When I tried to put my foot down, I couldn't—not without crying out in wild pain.

Mom and Dad rushed me to the emergency room, where a pediatrician, stumped, referred them to an orthopedic doctor. I wound up having physical therapy (PT), mostly the stretching and massaging of my legs, for an hour a week. It was painful. Worse, it didn't work. No amount of stretching could change the scary things that were happening to me. I was morphing.

One-year-old me at my home in Antigua

Even after a year of therapy, my left side was folded, my neck was jammed into my left shoulder, my limbs were pushed together and I became small, squinched in.

Blowing out the candles with Mom on my second birthday

The part of my brain that controlled walking, running, reaching, stretching, climbing, speaking, hugging—all motor skills—was in trouble. The doctors in Antigua did their best, but they weren't able to help much. For starters, they couldn't pinpoint why my body had gone haywire.

Our fun-in-the-sun island didn't have world-class medical facilities, so my parents looked to the States. In the fall of 2003 Mom got a six-month leave of absence from her job and got herself and me ready for a big journey.

On November 1, 2003, we were on a flight to New York.

Just in time for one of its coldest winters.

3
NYC

Before I was born my parents had visited the Big Apple a few times, loving the bright lights, the busy-busy, and the everything-everything all the time. When Mom and I arrived in 2003, though, the only thing she cared about was getting me some help. We had a place to stay, thanks to fellow Antiguan Keden Turner, a friend of a friend, who lived near Yankee Stadium in the Bronx. This *Angel* (what I call folks who've given the Philip family heaps of help) let us have a room in his sixth-floor apartment, where he hardly ever stayed. This was awesome and generous, but it came with a problem.

The building had no elevator. Mom had to become SuperMom. Whenever we went anywhere, she had to carry me in my stroller up and down five flights of stairs.

Up and down those stairs for errands because she had nobody to mind me.

Up and down those stairs to get me a special kind of health insurance so I could get medical care in this country, which led to more up and down those five flights of stairs for Mom to get me to doctor's appointments. At one of those appointments, I was finally diagnosed with something a doctor in Antigua had thought was a possibility, something my parents did not want to hear. No, my body was not experiencing some temporary glitch. I had the incurable CP, cerebral palsy.

The type of CP that had its grip on me was spastic quadriplegia. That meant that my arms and legs could only make stiff and jerky movements. On top of that, my left arm would get tighter and tighter over time. I'd never be able to fully extend it.

My CP meant I would never walk, let alone run. I'd spend hours upon hours a day in a stroller and eventually in a wheelchair, unable to stand unless I used leg braces or was strapped into a stander.

My CP meant that whenever I needed to get from my bed to my chair, or from my chair to the toilet, somebody would have to help me for the rest of my life.

Because of CP I would never be able to take big, deep breaths and never be able to clear my lungs because of the way my body contorted, and the weakness of my chest muscles. So for me, getting a common cold could be a dangerous thing. It could develop into bronchitis or pneumonia because of the tough time I have coughing up phlegm.

My CP would cause me mind-blowing pain sometimes. Pain from not being able to move or shift my body. Pain from my muscles tightening—sometimes tightening so much that I would need some massaging or gentle rocking to loosen up muscles so I could extend an arm, a wrist, a finger. But even when I wasn't in intense pain, I'd always be kind of uncomfortable from spending so much time seated. If you have your mobility, imagine you're on a twelve- or sixteen-hour plane ride. Then imagine that during that journey you can't get up—not once—to stretch your legs, your back, your arms. Now imagine making that journey day after day, year in, year out. Well, that's me.

And cold weather—big problemo! When people with mobility are cold, I am *freezing* and my limbs get even stiffer. Since I can't move much, I don't generate a lot of body heat. Though I don't remember being three years old, I can totally imagine the shock I must have felt that first winter in NYC, going from year-round heat to so much cold.

I faced that cold almost every day because Mom had enrolled me in a preschool for kids with disabilities at Manhattan's Roosevelt Hospital. That's where I made my first American friends: Calvin, Dante, Moesha, and Natalie.

Along with the usual ABCs and 123s, I got physical therapy in pre-K. In addition to having my limbs stretched, I also started doing standing exercises to strengthen my legs, as well as exercises on a triangular bolster thing to build up my back muscles.

There was also occupational therapy (OT), to help me do my "jobs." What jobs does a three-year-old have? At that point, mainly playing, feeding myself, and brushing my teeth. Along with getting a lot of practice holding and navigating objects, I also played hand-eye coordination games to amp up my ability to focus.

As they say on TV: but wait, there's more!

Twice a week I had speech therapy, which included chewing gum (yum!) to train my tongue to move properly. I had to say long sentences to boost breathing stamina. "My dad and little brother live in Antigua, while I live with Mom in New York." That's the kind of sentence I had to work on. I often had to stop midway to catch my breath.

And, man, those words that start with *c*, *s*, or *z*! My lisp was my biggest problem. To this day I have trouble with words like *scream* and *sweet*. I used to get really uptight and embarrassed about all that, but I can happily report that I have learned to love my lisp.

With Mom taking care of me full-time, our family now only had one breadwinner, Dad. By day he worked in sales and marketing at an importing company, and every other night as a government inspector at different casinos on the island. Dad also had a third job: being daddy to a second son. When Mom and I left Antigua, I had a nearly five-month-old little brother: Aren Brandon St. Clare Philip, born June 13, 2003.

With Dad working so much, Aren spent a lot of time with Maria Isaac, who was like a grandmother to us. Over the years Granny Maria and her son, Algen, my godfather, were about the only people in Antigua Mom and Dad could turn to for support. Both Mom's and Dad's parents were dead, and they weren't really close to the family they still had on the island.

Meanwhile, back in NYC . . . Mom eventually got a break from all the up and down stairs with me. In February we moved to Harlem, where one of Dad's nieces, Arah, had an apartment on Edgecombe Avenue. And (yay!) Arah's building had an elevator. As her apartment was a one bedroom, Angel Arah put us up in her living room. There, Mom and I slept on a queen-size air bed. Just like when we lived in the Bronx, Mom, the most organized person I know, spent most of her Saturdays cooking up about a week's worth of food for us, continuing to bring me up on the tastes of Antigua.

As a little kid, of course I had no idea whatsoever what was going on, no idea of the sacrifices SuperMom was making for me.

Loss of income.

Separation from Dad and my baby brother, Aren.

Being in a city where she didn't know heaps of people.

Learning to navigate the city above- and below-ground, along with school rules and social services.

All the while, like Dad, Mom was convinced that I had a lot of potential. Try everything before you give up. That's the way they think. And they believed that I could fly.

The big question at the time was: When Mom's leave was up, would we fly back to Antigua? Mom was so grateful for the first-rate care I was getting and she did not want it to end. But there was a problem. I was getting heavier. If Mom got another leave or if she quit her job and found a way to stay in America, could she really continue to take care of me? All by herself?

Something had to give.

4
TRADING PLACES

About a month after Mom and I landed in NYC, Dad came to see us. As soon as Dad laid eyes on Mom, he got all busted up inside.

Mom looked horrible, Dad said. She had lost a *lot* of weight. Lydia Philip was Stress Central. Up and down those stairs. Up and down those stairs. Even after we moved to Edgecombe Avenue, she continued to have quite a bit of up and down with me in my stroller when taking me somewhere by bus or subway. Plus, winter in the Big Apple is no joke for somebody used to year-round heat.

Between Dad's December 2003 visit and spring 2004, my parents decided that they would trade places when Mom's leave was up. Dad would take care of me up in NYC. Mom would take care of Aren in Antigua. I knew nothing about this plan. All I knew is that when Dad showed up in early April 2004 with my baby brother, my family was together again (yay!). But there was an ouch for Mom. Aren, now ten months old, didn't know who she was.

Yes, that hurt, but Mom handled it. She was in much better shape to do so. By then she had more peace of mind and was more settled, more adapted to New York City living than she had been in December when we'd last seen my dad. Still, there was no denying that I was a growing boy. I'd only get heavier. Dad was fully committed to becoming my main caretaker.

Good jobs, good income. Dad had decided to give it all up. For Mom's sake. For mine.

Dad said I was in great shape too, except for . . . yep, another curveball in Aaronland, another problemo. It was something Mom never detected because she slept like a rock.

Not Dad. He had a hard time getting used to our air bed. He tossed and turned all night. Thanks to his sleeplessness he noticed that my breathing was strange. Stop and start. Stop and start.

"Lydia! Lydia!" Dad woke Mom up. "Aaron's not breathing."

No way, thought Mom.

Yes way. She soon heard my stop-and-start breathing too.

Our pediatrician confirmed what my parents thought—that I had sleep apnea—and gave us a referral to an ear, nose, and throat doctor. About two weeks after that doctor saw me, I had my tonsils shaved, my first surgery. It took about two hours, and after a day of recovery I was good to go. Except there was no SuperMom to comfort me. By then, she and Aren had gone back to Antigua.

I didn't know they were leaving until two or three days before their flight. To soften the blow they told me that Mom was going back to clear some things up so that she and Aren could return and stay for good. It didn't work. And I was the type of kid who could throw a tantrum for hours. They say I pitched a really big fit—cried, kicked, screamed—when Mom and Aren left. I later learned that Mom cried for the whole five-hour flight from America to Antigua.

I was three years old.

5
LIKE CHRISTMAS

Several months after Mom and Aren returned to Antigua, Dad and I moved out of Angel Arah's place and into our own little place, on Colgate Avenue in the Bronx. It was in the Soundview section, once home to hip-hop legend Afrika Bambaataa, Supreme Court Justice Sonia Sotomayor, and (yikes!) serial killer David Berkowitz, aka Son of Sam.

When I said Dad and I had our own *little* place, I meant it. It was a tiny studio apartment in the basement of a house that belonged to a cousin of Mom's. It was a damp little place. Damp like Dad's spirits most days, I later learned.

Dad had too much free time on his hands and it drove him crazy. He *so* missed working! With only a nonimmigrant visa, it wasn't easy for him to get a job, even a part-time job. He maybe could have picked up day work with a construction crew, but for those jobs you usually have to be up and out at the crack of dawn. Dad couldn't do that because he had no one to take care of me in the mornings. Had I been a normal kid, that probably would have been less of a problem. Of course, had I been a normal kid, our family wouldn't have been half in America, half in Antigua. And Dad would not have been in the scary position of living off of his and Mom's savings and wondering how long the money would last before some miracles came our way. Still, day after day Dad put on a brave front and a happy face for me.

In his war on boredom, Dad became something of a foodie—watching cooking shows, surfing the net for recipes and menus, cooking new and different things.

(He made a mean stewed Angus beef.) I'm sure that Dad becoming Chef Petrone is the reason I am keen on eating all kinds of food now. (I'll try just about anything once—like sushi, now one of my favorite foods.)

On weekends Dad and I went out and stayed out if the weather wasn't horrible. Just like when we lived in Manhattan, we spent a lot of time in parks. Colgate Close Park. Soundview Park. Van Cortlandt Park. If it was a play park, Dad carefully and expertly had me get some exercise on swings, monkey bars, and slides. (If you have your mobility, you probably can't appreciate how much everyday physical exercise contributes to your growth and development—strengthening your bones, improving your coordination, etc.)

Come Monday, Dad's days went back to dreary. He swears that computer video chat software saved his life! He and Mom were able to talk face-to-face every day.

In April 2005, a year after Mom and Dad traded places, I was back in the hospital for another operation. My hamstrings this time. This surgery was to keep my

Playing in the snow with Dad in New York

knees from freezing in a crouch position, so I could sit in a posture closer to normal. During the five-hour surgery some muscles (dead ones) on the backs of my thighs were cut away to ease the tension and the tightening.

When I woke up, I found my legs in casts to straighten them out, casts I had on for about three weeks. Whatever pain and discomfort I felt while I healed was dulled because Mom was with me—*live*, in the flesh! She arrived before the surgery and stayed for about a month. With her was Aren, now nearly two.

Mom and Aren's visits were the best, most wonderful pick-me-ups. She did everything in her power to come see us twice a year. Sometimes she stayed for two weeks. Sometimes she stayed longer.

The minute I spotted her and Aren at the airport or when Dad opened our apartment door, that "missing feeling" faded away. Mom's hugs and kisses had healing power, I swear! Once my brother and I started playing together, it was like we had never been apart.

Every visit was like Christmas. One year the visit was at Christmastime—best present in the world! I remember us sitting around a big white Christmas tree. I remember us eating good food and listening to holiday tunes. I also remember Aren and me playing video games on our Nintendo DSs until way past our bedtime.

I knew that their visits were just that, visits, but I tried not to think about them leaving. When the dreaded day came, I was a mess, a wreck. I was in Torture City!

It hurt so bad to see them go! Up and down. Those visits had me up and down.

It was like Christmas again when Dad and I went to Antigua. Those trips also had me up and down, up and down.

It was during our first trip back, in the summer of 2004, that I learned to do something one therapist said was impossible.

6
A BREAKTHROUGH
& SOME BUBBLY FOR ME

One of my pre-K teachers tried to potty train me. So did Dad. They both kind of stopped after a therapist at my school kept insisting that I couldn't be potty trained and would spend the rest of my life in diapers.

Despite what the therapist said, SuperMom refused to abandon Project Potty Train. During my eight-week stay in Antigua in the summer of 2004, when I was a little over three years old, Mom took me to the bathroom one day. In full woman-on-a-mission mode, she sat me down on the toilet, put pillows between my back and the toilet top, then waited.

And waited.

And waited.

The wait was so long that she dozed off right where she sat on the bathroom floor.

"Mommy! Something's coming!" I screamed after about an hour.

You guessed it. I pooped. Gross? Not at all. Not for me. It was a great accomplishment. No more diaper life for me!

So proud of me, SuperMom threw me a party to celebrate my achievement. And that party was not premature. During the rest of my time in Antigua I was diaper-free. Mom says I never had an accident. Not one.

During my next summer in Antigua, another miracle came my way.

Mom didn't like the idea of my PT being put on hold while I was in Antigua. She asked around and learned about Sua, a Chinese therapist in St. John's. Sua worked in Redcliffe Quay, one of St. John's oldest neighborhoods.

One day on our way to therapy, we bumped into a man who had a shop downstairs from Sua. I gave this man a cheerful hello, then bombarded him with questions.

What did he do?

Where was he from?

What did he know about Sua?

I was fascinated with Sua. By then I was hooked on anime and so crazy about all things Asian.

I can't remember everything I asked that stranger in Redcliffe Quay that day, but I gotta believe I had way more than three questions for him. I was quite the motormouth and bursting with curiosity about everything and everybody. I have my parents to thank for that. Mom and Dad bought me loads of educational toys. Plus, they talked to me and read to me a lot when I was a baby—starting when I was in that incubator. Anyway, as I got older, it wasn't at all odd for me to ask strangers questions.

That stranger in Redcliffe Quay was curious too. About me. Why couldn't I walk? After a bit of conversation with Mom and Dad, he went his way and we went ours. Then about three weeks later, when it was just Dad and me on our therapy outing, we bumped into that man again. This time he and Dad had a longer conversation. And it led to something really wonderful.

About two months after Dad and I returned to New York, Mom got a call from that man. He wanted to help me—to see to it that I got a new kind of therapy with a doctor he knew in Boston. This Angel, who became a family friend, was the famous jewelry designer Hans Smit. (His shop in Redcliffe Quay, Goldsmitty, is a major tourist destination.)

On top of having an amazing jewelry-designing mind, Angel Hans also has a huge heart. He was president of Antigua's Hourglass Foundation, which does loads of charitable work, like creating a drug and alcohol rehab center (with help from Eric Clapton).

Every year, come Christmas, the Hourglass Foundation has a major fund raiser: a big Champagne Party at Nelson's Dockyard. Some of the proceeds from the Champagne Party of 2005 were earmarked for my new treatment: injections of Botulinum toxin type A, aka Botox.

Family and friends at my fund raiser at Nelson's Dockyard in Antigua

No, I didn't have wrinkles, but I did have all that stiffness and tightness in my hands and legs. Botox is a muscle relaxant and it's not just for people who want to get rid of their wrinkles. If some of my muscles were more relaxed, then they could be stretched farther and more easily.

Starting around March 2006, every three months Dad took me up to Boston so Angel Hans's doctor friend could inject Botox into the tendons of my left arm and hamstrings in my left leg. The injections were sometimes mildly painful. At other times they were make-you-wanna-holler painful. "No Pain, No Gain" could be my middle name.

While I certainly didn't look forward to those Botox injections, I did look forward to going to Boston because we had family there: Dad's brother Nixson,

Me and Uncle Nixson

who had moved to the States in the 1990s, and his American wife, Shirley. Before our Boston-for-Botox trips we didn't see them often. Now we got to see them each time we headed north. It was so nice to be around more family. During one trip, Angel Aunt Shirley gave me a party for my fifth birthday!

Birthday party at Chuck E. Cheese's!

Boston trips became rare after about a year, when the grant money from the Hourglass Foundation ran out. My insurance didn't cover the treatment. Medicaid did, but I wasn't eligible for that because I wasn't a US citizen. So it was bye-bye Botox. Bummer.

Even so, by the time my Boston-for-Botox days ended I had definitely moved up in the world.

7
MSC

"Hello, my new friends!"

That was me in the fall of 2006. I was greeting my classmates on the first day of kindergarten, so happy to be in Big Kid School! And right away, I did the Name Thing, just as I had done in pre-K and have done most of my life when meeting someone for the first time. That is, I had to let everybody know that my name isn't pronounced AIR-un (that's my brother Aren) but AY-ron (think A-Rod).

I was schooling people on my name at Manhattan School for Children, aka P.S. 333, aka MSC, on

Being silly with a friend at the Manhattan School for Children

Manhattan's Upper West Side. When I started at MSC, it had about six hundred students, and many of them were the children of professionals, people of means and resources. That meant MSC had a lot of extra support.

Another thing that MSC had going for it was Integrated Co-Teaching (ICT) classes. Instead of shunting kids with physical disabilities into classes of their own, kids like me got to learn alongside kids with no physical or mental challenges. The curriculum and the classwork, like the configuration of these classrooms, were designed with the needs of children with disabilities in mind.

I was at MSC thanks to my pre-K teacher Lori Harrington and a nice school-placement lady at the New York City Department of Education (DOE). Angel Lori pleaded—even to the point of tears—that I be an exception to the rule that kids had to go to a school in their district. She didn't think I could maximize my potential at any school in my district in the Bronx. Had I known what was going on, I'm sure I would have seconded that. I was ready for my potential to be maximized.

One of my first and favorite toys was a Leapster, a gift from another early Angel in my life: my godmother, Brenda Emmanuel. She gave me that Leapster for Christmas in 2003 so I could occupy my mind with spelling, memorizing things, and doing sing-a-longs. When other kids were ripping and running (or trying to), I was often in my stroller or on the couch playing math and language games and doing puzzles on my Leapster. (Legend has it that at a very young age, I was tossing out words like *film* and *vacuum*.) My Leapster also had really fun games that helped me with hand-eye coordination and with my mental and physical stamina. There were drawing games too. One time I almost banged the life out of that Leapster, that's how frustrated I was over not being able to draw a heart. I know that Leapster had a lot to do with why I was a bit ahead of some pre-K peers. The Leapster may also have sparked my interest in art.

Anyway . . . having convinced Dad that MSC would be ideal for me, Angel Lori also succeeded in convincing the DOE lady. *Presto!* I got into one of NYC's best public schools, where so many more Angels would come into my life. Like my kindergarten teachers, Lisa Pomerantz and Mia Kargen.

On the first day of school I sat in Angel Lisa's lap and refused to budge. I could be quite the stubborn kid. While Angel Lisa was all soft, cuddly love, Angel Mia was tough love—just what the doctor ordered for a stubborn temper-tantrum-prone kid like me. Those coteachers were ideal for me.

There were also Debra Fisher and Mary Antony, my OTs. Boy, did they have their work cut out for them. Even after all my OT in pre-K, my CP was so bad that I was close to not being able to hold anything in my hands. I even had trouble reaching for things.

At first Angels Deb and Mary did things like simply place one of their hands several inches over my head and say, "Reach up to here." It took me a long time to get it. I had to think really hard about how to move ("motor planning"). Then one day they tried something different. Holding a beanbag above my head, one of them said, "Grab this beanbag," and I got it—fast! Why? Because I liked the way that beanbag felt in my hands. I actually had a will and urge to hold it. So I did.

I was even more gung ho to gain control over my hands after Angel Deb one day asked me what I most wanted to do.

Draw.

Draw.

Then draw some more.

At that point I couldn't make a crayon or pencil

go where I wanted it to go and do what I wanted it to do. Scribble scrabble was all I produced. Plus, there was the problem with my left hand. I couldn't make it hold the paper down while my right hand made that scribble scrabble. Result: the images of people and animals, flowers and veggies, monsters and ghosts stayed trapped inside my head.

With help from Angels Lisa and Mia, Angels Deb and Mary worked their magic to get my floppy, jerky right hand to maneuver a pencil or crayon, modifying materials and tools along the way. Dad says I was making progress after a few months but that it was more than a year before I drew anything that made any sense. All I remember is how good it felt to get those images out of my head and on to paper and in full color. (Solution to the paper-positioning problem: whoever was with me taped it down or placed something heavy on it.)

More than anything else I wanted to make anime art. "I'm going to do this!" I vowed one day. The *Sesame Street* gang had held my attention for a while, but after

I saw anime characters—Bert and Ernie, move over! Those anime eyes really grabbed me. Pokémon was definitely one of my obsessions that got me hooked on anime; although Dad said that when I was a baby in Antigua, he and I watched a lot of *Dragon Ball Z*, so maybe it really started there. When I got old enough to surf the net, I spent hours, I mean *hours,* hunting down anime shows. Nerd hideouts, chat rooms—you name it, I went wherever I had to go to feed my anime addiction.

While I was on my way to being able to create anime (and learning math, language arts, and other stuff), my CP meant that during my school days, along with OT three times a week, I had PT three times a week in MSC's Blue Sky Room. In that blue-painted activity room, with fluffy white clouds on the walls, my body was treated to stretching, balancing, and sitting games. I also spent time on a red wedge to strengthen my trunk and bear weight on my arms.

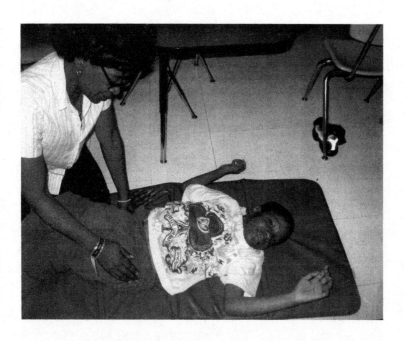

Working with a paraprofessional at school

My CP meant that, just as in pre-K, I would need a paraprofessional (para) to get my outerwear off when I arrived at school and then back on at the end of the day. The para would have to do a bunch of other stuff like hand me things while in class; take me to the bathroom; and get me in and out of my wheelchair, my "desk" (an adaptive chair that helps my posture and so helps me function better), and my floor-seating system. (Maybe one day I'll write a song "Me and My Para" to the tune of "Me and My Shadow.")

And, oh yeah, my CP also meant spending about an hour every day in a stander, in the Blue Sky Room and at home. This was for the sake of my bones. If I didn't get the kind of weight-bearing exercise that people with mobility take for granted, my bones would get weaker, which can lead to bone fractures and osteoporosis. Thanks to that piece of equipment, I could stand and give my legs a little "workout."

When Mom and Aren came to visit Dad and me in the spring of 2009, my bones were the topic of much conversation.

8
FRIENDS HELPING FRIENDS

One of my doctors had told Dad that my hips might get weird. PT alone wouldn't be enough to combat the problem. That's not uncommon for people with CP. Because of muscle tightness and other complications, our hip bones can become misaligned—literally out of joint. I might need surgery, he said.

So that's why one September day in 2009, instead of being in school with my buds, I was in Montefiore Hospital having double hip surgery.

And I *really* needed that surgery: my left hip bone was out of its socket. The right hip bone was on the way to coming out. Messed-up hip bones meant my knees were turned in and touching. I wasn't in pain, exactly, but my body was getting so twisted. I hadn't been able to sleep comfortably on my stomach in ages.

The surgery lasted between five and six hours. And (yay!) it was successful, but the aftermath was not. When I came to about a half hour later, in hip-to-knee casts, I was out of my mind with pain. It was the WORST pain I had ever experienced. Dad said he had never seen such uncontrollable screaming—like I was a total lunatic. I didn't stop screaming until a double dose of morphine kicked in. After that, things were good in Aaronland.

A few days later Dad and I trooped up to Blythedale Children's Hospital in Valhalla, New York. Rehab time. Time for physical therapy and physical therapy, and then—yep, you guessed it—more physical therapy.

I think I was in Blythedale's Therapy Village for rehab one Saturday when someone we knew slightly spotted Dad sitting on a couch, waiting for me.

It was Dr. Laurette Olson, a professor at Mercy College in Dobbs Ferry, New York, about twenty minutes from Blythedale. Dr. Olson taught in Mercy's Graduate Program in OT. Her courses included class trips to Blythedale, so that her students could meet with kids like me.

Dad and I had met Dr. Olson a couple of times at MSC when there were speakers for teachers, families, and the community about topics related to OT. My dad liked to go to these events and I would go with him. Naturally, when she sighted Dad at Blythedale, Dr. Olson came over to find out how we were doing.

How was Dad managing to get back and forth from NYC to Valhalla?

Answer: he wasn't going back and forth that much. Dad had given up our second apartment in the Bronx, on Tremont Avenue, which was another place without an elevator. Thank goodness we lived on the second floor. Every time we needed to go out, Dad had to take my wheelchair apart and make three trips down to the ground floor.

After Dad reassembled my chair, he went back up those stairs to our apartment to carry me down and get me into my chair. When we returned home, Dad went through the same thing in reverse. I remember how very tired he looked after he got my chair and me into our apartment. I felt so bad, but there was nothing else he could do. (I wished hard for a jet pack!)

But Dad hadn't given up that Tremont Avenue apartment because of the stairs—he did it because the rent was a killer.

My parents' savings had dwindled really far down. Though by now Dad had a green card, he hadn't landed a steady job. His work life was unpredictable, like he'd have a few weeks of temp work, or occasional construction work from a friend. This was in the fall of 2009, and things were bad for lots of folks because of the financial crisis. There were layoffs and cutbacks everywhere. Jobs were really hard to come by.

Dad knew that after my surgery I'd be in Blythedale for about three months; since the hospital let parents stay with their children, Dad decided to save on rent money by putting our stuff in storage and moving in with me, sleeping in a fold-out chair next to my bed.

On days when Dad had construction work, he had to get to the city at about seven in the morning. And he had quite the trek. First a short walk down a hill to a bus that would take him on the twenty-five- to forty-minute ride to the Metro-North station in White Plains, followed by a fifteen- to fifty-minute train ride south, depending on where the job site was.

On days his friend had no work for him, Dad hung out with me at Blythedale, learning more about massage and stretching techniques. Learning more about my CP.

As Dad and Dr. Olson talked on, she noticed that he looked a bit thin.

"What are you doing for meals?" she asked. Dr. Olson knew the hospital like the back of her hand. Not only did she bring her students there, she had also done research at the hospital. So she knew the cafeteria was closed on weekends and that the only food available in the building came from vending machines. She also knew that down the hill from Blythedale there were convenience stores and places to grab a slice.

So what was my dad doing for meals?

Answer: Surviving on my leftovers, mostly.

Dr. Olson returned the next day with a cooler full of ready-to-eat and microwavable food. Naturally, she was immediately upgraded to Angel status. It wasn't just the food. It was the *way* she gave it. So casual about the help. She even gave Dad rides to the train sometimes, or helped him out with a MetroCard here and there when he went job hunting after the construction work dried up. When we thanked her, she shrugged it off. As far as she was concerned it was no biggie, just a case of a friend helping friends.

Friend helping friends wasn't a one-way street, though. One day Angel Dr. Laurie needed some help from us. And we were more than happy to give it.

9
MERCY

For years Dr. Laurie had been giving her students an awesome opportunity: she arranged for these future OTs to actually meet with the kinds of kids they would be working with one day. She knew that these men and women needed more than textbook knowledge, more than theory. They needed real live interaction with people with CP or other disabilities.

While I was still recuperating at Blythedale, Dr. Laurie one day invited my dad and me to come down to Therapy Village where she was working with her students. I talked to them about what it was like to be a child with CP. My dad told them what it was like to raise a child with CP. They were so cool and I had fun talking to them. I told them jokes and made them laugh. Some of them even came back at the end of the day to see me in my room and brought me toys. When I was finally back in action, Dr. Laurie invited Dad and me to come to Mercy College and speak with her students. (I even got a speaker's fee!)

Our visits to Mercy became an annual event. Dr. Laurie's students got to learn a lot about Aaronland.

Over the years I would tell future OTs what makes a great para: someone who can anticipate my needs—like taking notes for me in classes, making sure supplies and things I can handle are within easy reach, stuff like that.

I would tell future OTs about how hard it is sometimes to keep up in class with children who don't have disabilities because a teacher might be going too fast or because the size of my chair prevents me from seeing something up front on the board or because I'm experiencing some pain and discomfort.

I would tell them about my academic strengths (reading and writing—yay!) and weaknesses (math—grrrr!).

I told one group about a time when I had a ton of difficulty with my stander because my knees hurt so bad and how things only got better after my dad started giving me knee rubs every night at bedtime.

I would also tell future OTs about my passions and hobbies, from anime to writing takeoffs on classic stories like *Alice in Wonderland*. I was really into fantasy stories then, and later devoured the Percy Jackson series. But even my favorite books threw another curveball in Aaronland.

It's tough for me to read a physical book because you need both hands to keep it balanced, and my left hand won't cooperate. Sometimes my para or my dad would put paper clips or binder clips between the pages to keep the book steady, but that barely worked. Reading became less of a production after Dad gave me an e-reader one Christmas. Of course once you start with new technology, you are never satisfied and want more. That was me (and I guess every other kid in America). I wanted to read my ebooks, but I also wanted fun apps, a camera, my music. . . . A few years later I was in heaven when one of my Angels upgraded me to a sweet new device that could do it all. By then I was pretty much done with fantasy and was all about biographies and love stories.

Anyway: got off track there. Back to Mercy.

During my first presentation at Mercy College in December 2010, I showed future OTs how I roll—literally. I wheeled myself back and forth, from student to student. Slow. Fast. I bragged that I could pop a wheelie. I wish! I couldn't really, but I did show them my version of the moonwalk (sorta).

After showing off a bit and acting zany I took questions. Don't judge my answers—I was only nine!

"I want to know, what do you like to do for fun with your friends?"

Answer: "Draw *and* be silly!" (Like I said, I was nine. . . .)

"When you eat do you use regular forks and—"

Answer: "Yeah, like regular eatingware."

"Did it take you a long time to learn how to use your new wheelchair?"

Answer: "No, not at all."

My wheelchair had been a long time coming.

By 2008 I had outgrown the first motorized chair I got in 2004 while in pre-K. Insurance rigmarole led to delay after delay. During the wait, MSC arranged for a loaner that I nicknamed my EIB (the initials of a classmate it had belonged to). About a month before my first presentation at Mercy in December 2010, my new wheelchair finally came. That's why I was wheeling around that classroom like a maniac. It felt *so* good to have that new chair. New wheelchair, new possibilities. With my new chair I could raise myself up to be level with a high table. Also when I was feeling sleepy on a bus, or anywhere else, I could tilt back and relax. Ahhh. . . .

As I wheeled around the classroom that December day, those grad students also learned a bit about how

I got dressed; about my dream of being an anime cartoonist; how bonkers I was over *The Marvelous Misadventures of Flapjack* and *SpongeBob SquarePants*, my two favorite TV shows; and that with my right index finger I could keyboard faster than I could write. I told them, too, about how we used to go to Antigua and that one of the best things about my time there was when Dad took me to the beach and buried my legs in the sand.

The interest these students had in my life really amazed me. And I have to say that I was sometimes surprised to see how little OTs-in-training knew about some of the things kids with disabilities have to deal with. And thanks to my Mercy College talks I got a new Angel: Yvonne Rattray. After our first visit, on more than one occasion, Angel Yvonne got hold of a van and drove Dad and me up to Mercy and back.

I later learned that Dad and I got pretty high marks for our first presentation "Growing Up with CP & Parenting a Child with CP." Dr. Laurie's students had to fill out evaluation forms just like they had to for any other guest speaker. On that first visit to Mercy, all thirty-three students said they wanted to have us back.

"It was great to listen to a supportive father and a great, smart, motivated child," wrote one student. "It touched me in every kind of way."

"Firstly," began another student, "I was so surprised by the verbal skills he displayed." ("He" was me, of course.)

Yet another student wrote: "We got a realistic sense of what it is like to have a disabled child, and that this father has found a generally callous attitude when trying to get help."

I don't remember what that was about specifically, but I do remember callous people over the years. I remember people on city buses sucking their teeth or rolling their eyes because the bus had to spend a little more time at a stop so Dad could get me on board. I remember people on subways getting annoyed over how much space my wheelchair took up. *People! People! People!* I sometimes wanted to holler, *Do you think we have a limo and simply refuse to use it?! Do you think we have buckets of money and just refuse to spend it on cabs?*

UGH!

Those Mercy College students I met in December 2010 were not one bit callous—they were some of the warmest and most sensitive people I've ever met. Even so, I kind of wanted to sink through the floor after a question that one student asked, totally unaware that it was a sore spot for Dad and me.

This question came after I mentioned that I couldn't have friends come over to my house. When the student asked why, I froze. I turned to Dad for a lifeline, for some signal as to how I should respond. Was it OK to tell the truth?

Finally, Dad nodded.

I wheeled over to the young woman and whispered, "I live in a shelter."

I was a lousy whisperer. I think half the class heard me.

10
HARD TIMES

We had spent Christmas 2009 in Blythedale. A few days after that my casts came off, so when we rang in the new year we had at least one bit of good news to celebrate. But Dad still had no job and we had no place to live. At one point he thought after I rehabbed, maybe we should just pack it in and return to Antigua where we still had a home. But no, he couldn't do that. I was getting such good care in America.

One day a social worker at Blythedale asked Dad if he had tried to get into a shelter.

"Shel-who? Shel-what?" That was Dad. He knew

nothing about shelters. In Antigua, homeless people could usually find someplace to stay. (Once Mom took in a single mother with a bunch of kids, letting them live in our home until the woman could get back on her feet.) If a homeless person couldn't find anyone to take him or her in, Antigua has warm weather all the time. Camping out beneath the stars is not as terrible as it would be in New York City during the winter.

In January 2010, with the help of some Angels, Dad learned to navigate the shelter system. A few days before I was to be discharged from Blythedale, Dad was told that there was a place for us. It was in a building on 125th Street near Broadway. We were given an apartment on the fourth floor. It was déjà vu all over again. No elevator.

One of our Angels came to our rescue once more. She lit a fire under somebody because within two days Dad got a call that Hale House had a place for us. And Hale House had an elevator. Another good thing about Hale House: it was on West 113th Street and my school was on West 93rd. On a good day Dad and I could get to and from school in about twenty minutes.

I always felt sorry for the homeless. When I was little, I used to ask Dad to give a dollar to homeless people we passed on the street. Of course I never expected to *be* a homeless person. It felt so weird and scary. And no visitors? Dad and I never had loads of folks who wanted to visit us, but knowing that visitors were forbidden made me feel yucky.

I don't remember much about Hale House. It's like the part of my brain where those memories are stored got a military-grade data wipe. Mostly I remember meetings with counselors. There seemed to be an excessive number of them. I remember being uncomfortable at those meetings and wanting the counselors to just go away. Looking back, I know the meetings were to help Dad and me. There was help with money management, for example. And, thankfully, soon after we moved into Hale House, Dad had some money to manage. He got a job. It came so out of the blue.

Months earlier Dad had had an interview with SchoolFood (the Department of Education's Office of School Food program). This was thanks to Penny Dow, mom of my classmate Cookie. Had Angel Penny not helped Dad sign up to work for SchoolFood, that interview never would have happened. But what a letdown it was for Dad when after the interview—nothing.

Dad was shocked and amazed when, not long after we moved into Hale House, he got a call from a woman at SchoolFood.

Was he still interested in the job?

"Can I start now?" Dad replied.

No, but soon. Dad started working for the DOE in February 2010 and would wind up—so convenient for us—working in the cafeteria of MSC.

As part of getting people on the path out of homelessness, Hale House required you to save a portion of your income. As Dad recalls, he had to put two hundred dollars a month into a savings account. Every three months he had to show a counselor his savings-account statement. Often after Dad did that, he withdrew a chunk of the money and sent it to Antigua. Disaster had struck again.

About six months after Dad and I moved into Hale House and Dad got a job, Mom lost her job. Along with her regular job, for years she had been doing event planning (mostly weddings) on the side. But that side job didn't bring in enough money to support Mom and my brother, Aren.

Until Mom found another job, things were supertight. Their savings were gone. Plus, in the winter of 2009, to get Dad and me through those early days of the Great Recession, my parents had sold a small house in Antigua that they had been renting out. That money only went so far, even with Dad economizing. There was no eating out. There were no new clothes. Dad bought nothing that wasn't an absolute necessity. At school, I was a clean-plate boy at breakfast and at lunch.

Just as Dad and I were living hand to mouth, so were Mom and Aren after she lost her job. Things got so bad that, for a time, Mom and Aren were living off the pomegranate, soursop, and other fruit trees on our land, and off other food that Mom grew during the rainy season. That home, which had no mortgage, was the only asset my parents had left. They were determined to hold on to it. If push really came to shove, if Dad and I had to pack up and pack it in, at least we'd still have a home in Antigua.

Hard times in America. Hard times in Antigua.

And I was having a very hard time in school.

11
CATI

I was too embarrassed to tell anyone at school that Dad and I lived in a shelter, but I slipped up one day and told a friend, a boy I'd known since kindergarten. Soon my whole class found out; then the whole school, I guess.

My homelessness became school news in 2011, when I was ten. Worst of all, it happened at the start of the day. It was when each class had a meet-up, gathering in a circle. It was bonding/community-building time. A question usually kicked it off.

On that worst day of my life, the question was, "If

you could wish for one thing to happen to someone, what would it be?"

My friend since kindergarten said something like, "I wish Aaron didn't live in a homeless shelter."

I wanted to die! I tried to contain myself, but I couldn't. Right there in front of everybody I started screaming and crying. It was pretty bad.

I wanted to die! It was no consolation to know that my friend hadn't meant to embarrass me, that he had only wanted me to have a home again.

I wanted to die! The teachers had a heck of a time calming me down.

Yes, MSC had a diverse student body. Yes, it preached inclusion and had inclusion classes. Yes, I had so many opportunities at MSC I probably never would have had at another school. Yes, I was included in school plays and other events. Yes, I was often chosen to greet a distinguished visitor to our school (like the Princess of Denmark in 2011).

All good and wonderful things. Still, I felt like an outsider. It wasn't just about my CP. (And being black in a mostly white school was the least of my problems—and really not a problem at all.) The problem was that most of my schoolmates lived on the Upper West Side and I had lived mostly in the Bronx. (And when I lived on the Upper West Side it was in a shelter that didn't allow visitors.)

Added to that, unlike many of my schoolmates, I was poor. And now everybody knew how *really* poor I was. Homeless.

The loneliness I felt that day is indescribable. It's a loneliness I would continue to feel year after year in school. And school was my world. It was the only place I had to be social. Unlike kids with mobility I didn't have that many opportunities to hang out with other kids outside of school.

It was hard to make friends in my neighborhood because I'm in a chair. It's hard for friendships to grow without being able to hang out after school or on weekends. Even if I wheeled up to some kids on my block or in a nearby park and just randomly started talking to them—well, it would be kind of awkward. There's a limit to how much we could really do together anyway. I would be on the sidelines watching them play ball, watching them skate, watching them ride bikes. I can't even do those friend-to-friend little things like a fist bump or a high five. Unless another kid was seated I was usually in the weird position of having to look up. Or talk to a waist.

Dad was doing everything in his power for us to *survive* in New York. He didn't really have the time or energy to set up playdates or help me make friends in the neighborhood.

MSC put a lot of emphasis on community and caring, but you can't make kids want to be friends with other kids. Can't make them invite other kids over for playdates. Can't make them invite other kids to birthday parties. The older I got, the fewer invites I got. Increasingly I felt Completely and Totally Invisible (CATI).

I always had a core group of buddies at MSC—Calvin, Sam, Jonah, Reuben, Lara, and Cookie. They actually went out of their way to make time to talk to me in the mornings before first class and during transitions between classes. But our friendship was limited because we lived so far apart (one lived out in Queens, then in Coney Island). And because money was always so tight, I wasn't able to join them in activities outside of school. The older I got, the harder it became to make new friends.

Like at recess. If I went outside mostly all I did was watch other kids tossing a football or having some other kind of physical fun.

Like at lunchtime. We kids with disabilities always sat at a table together. It wasn't far from where the "regular" kids ate, but it felt like we were on an island in the middle of an ocean. It wasn't a real school policy. I think it was probably something some paras decided. I have no idea why they wanted kids with disabilities to eat together. Maybe it was just easier? Maybe they wanted to protect us somehow? All I know is that it seemed totally ridiculous to me.

In the spring of 2012 I spoke up. I wheeled into my principal's office one day and asked if we kids with disabilities could sit wherever we wanted in the cafeteria. When she said yes, I was psyched.

A few months later, I was superhappy about something else: Dad and I finally moved out of Hale House and into an apartment in the Mount Eden section of the Bronx. Believe it or not, our day of independence from the shelter was July 4, 2012!

About a month later, I was beside myself with joy—ecstatic. The BEST THING EVER happened. My little brother, Aren, who had recently turned nine, came to America. Not for a visit, but to stay for good.

Just as I had been missing Aren, he had been missing me—and had in fact gone on strike. He refused to Skype with Dad and me if he had to live apart from us.

Aren's coming to America wasn't all about us having companionship. Mom was still jobless. She had no money for Aren's school fees. They were even living *without utilities*. Somehow she scraped together a hundred bucks to pay a flight attendant to accompany Aren up to the States.

Dad and me on Skype with my brother, Aren!

When Aren arrived, it was like nine birthdays and ten Christmases and a trip to the moon. We laughed and talked, laughed and talked nonstop. I was never so happy in all my life. Now I had a built-in friend. To play games. To bicker. To watch TV together. Because MSC had a sibling preference policy, Aren and I would go to school together. We were two peas in a pod, just like Mom had always wished. I have to believe our closeness started with our names.

Mom had chosen Aaron for me after she saw a movie

about Moses from the Bible. She felt a great admiration for his older brother, Aaron. She saw him as very courageous and liked that he helped his brother when he was tired and in doubt. She also liked the fact that Aaron was a peacemaker. When her second son came along, Mom wanted him to have a name as close as possible to mine.

Now that Aaron and Aren were brothers in arms, things were *so* much better in Aaronland.

And soon I'd start inviting even more people into Aaronland. . . .

12
AARONVERSE

Things didn't get much better after we kids with disabilities were free to sit wherever we wanted in the cafeteria. Sad to say, mostly we were ignored. And it's not like I didn't try. I'd usually wheel up to a table that had an empty space and be superfriendly. I'm used to having to make the extra effort to get people to talk to me.

Here's what mostly happened, though: After an awkward silence, one or more of the other kids might acknowledge my presence, but then they all went right back to whatever they'd been talking about, never looping me into the conversation. Sometimes I just sat there in silence. Other times I wheeled away. All the time I told Dad how lonely I felt at lunch, something I really didn't need to tell him. Because he worked in the cafeteria, he saw. Saw kids ignore me. Saw me reach out and get nothing in return. Saw the loneliness on my face. Why didn't I have lunch with my brother? He was only allowed to eat with his grade.

Dad and my Angels understood what I was going through, but many adults at my school just didn't get it. Some of them made me feel like after all MSC had done for me, I should shut my trap. It made me wonder if the generosity was conditional. Would it only come if I put on a happy-camper face? *All* the time? How could anyone take my feelings of loneliness and isolation as a sign of ingratitude? It was a hard lesson for me to learn: some people are great at pity but lousy at empathy.

In the spring of 2013 I decided, enough is enough! Enough of being CATI. I finally got it: Many of the kids at MSC simply didn't get me. And some probably didn't want to. I was tired of going out of my way to be upbeat, to initiate conversations, to bend over backward to make friends. (Not literally, of course.)

I started to realize that part of the problem wasn't just my CP or where I lived. I was different from most of my classmates in many other ways.

They liked Beyoncé. I liked music they knew nothing about, like FKA twigs and Sad Boys.

They talked about the latest Knicks game and I talked about anime.

They got bent out of shape about not being able to go outside for lunch. I got bent out of shape over the challenges people with disabilities face.

So I dreamed myself a new world of friends. I started my Tumblr blog: *Aaronverse*. I invited anyone and everyone to step into my world.

"Hi. My name is Aaron Philip. I'm in 6th grade, I'm in a wheelchair and I'm going to be sharing about how life is like in a wheelchair."

I told my audience of—one? two? zero?—that I wanted *Aaronverse* to be a place where other people who spend most of their days in wheelchairs could express themselves. I promised a once-a-week post on my day-to-day life in Aaronland. I ended that first post of under a hundred words with this: "I hope that you'll read this. THANK YOU!"

The next week, ripped from the headlines of my life, was my Sketchy Sunday ("5/19/13") post. How the one bright spot in my week, the cherry on my Sunday, was ruined. It was an art class at the Children's Museum of the Arts (CMA) in Manhattan. And it wasn't just any art class, but one with OTs on hand to help teacher-artists help kids like me manage supplies and tools. For example, taping colored pencils together for making stripes, and taping paper or canvas down on, say, a table.

OTs also made sure that teacher-artists understood that kids like me are easily distracted and taught them ways to help us stay focused on the fine points. That might be the use of a palette knife and how to mix colors, or which brush to use for watercolors and which to use for acrylics, or how to adjust from working on paper to working on canvas.

My classes at CMA only got better as I continued to make art and learn about different media and techniques, from Claymation to botanical drawing. The classes were also friendship-making and bonding sessions, with sibs and friends of all abilities welcome to participate. And talk about liberating! The emphasis was on *ability*—what people like me *can* do—not disability—what we *cannot* do. Though my brother wasn't as crazy about art as I was, he really enjoyed those classes too. (While I was dreaming of a career in the arts, Aren was torn between becoming a scientist or a football player.)

After I started those CMA art classes in the fall of 2012, we never missed one if we could help it. And we couldn't help it on the third Sunday in May 2013.

Access-A-Ride was supposed to pick up Dad, Aren, and me at 9:10 a.m.

9:15 a.m.: No Access-A-Ride

9:30 a.m.: Still no Access-A-Ride

10:00 a.m.: We were still outside our building.

Waiting—up in the Bronx with CMA way down in the Village. On a good day—meaning no crazy traffic or bad weather—it could take the Access-A-Ride driver thirty to forty-five minutes to get there. It could take way longer if that driver had a pickup after us.

10:15 a.m.: Access-A-Ride arrives. Already we were an hour late. And, yessiree, the driver had another pickup. Just my luck, the pickup was on the other side of the Bronx!

11:30 a.m. had come and gone when Access-A-Ride dropped the other passenger off I-don't-remember-where.

My class had started at 10:30 a.m. By the time we got to CMA, the class was over and out. We barely had enough time to say, "Hey!" to the staff and use the bathroom when Access-A-Ride pulled up right on time outside CMA to take us home.

Sketchy! Sketchy! Sketchy! My life is so full of unpredictables and simple things getting all complicated and stressful.

Like the day we had to take three buses to get home because the subway elevator was broken. What should have been about a thirty-minute subway ride took about three hours using the bus system. One broken elevator threw the rest of our day off. Dinner was later than normal. Getting ready for the next day was later than normal. Getting ready for bed was later than normal.

Sketchy!

Like not being able to take full advantage of my fluorescent-green Rifton ride, a souped-up trike for people like me. It was thanks to some Angels that Rifton donated this pricey ride with unique straps, pedals, handlebars, and other features that make it easy for me to get on it and, more important, stay on it. A Rifton ride really made my day. After Dad had me strapped in, I started pedaling with my right foot. After a while my left foot would catch and the momentum started. Soon I was zooming like crazy all over the neighborhood.

I could ride my trike along the sidewalks for forty-five minutes or an hour, with Dad fast walking and sometimes jogging alongside me, while Coach Aren on his green Razor scooter was on the other side or ahead of me, keeping me motivated. It often got so intense that I broke a sweat. Sometimes we had to make a pit stop so I could catch my breath.

Sadly, I never had the chance to enjoy my ride that much. Why? Because the elevator in our building is really small. Taking me out for a Rifton ride was like a second job for Dad. First he had to take the trike apart and bring it downstairs to the lobby. Then he had to come back up and get me. Once he got me to the lobby, he had to reassemble the trike, get me out of my chair and onto my ride, then put my chair in the laundry room and tape a sign on it— "THIS IS NOT GARBAGE!"—so security wouldn't take it to the basement.

After my really exhilarating ride, Dad had to go through the whole process of again taking the trike apart, then blah, blah, blah.

My Rifton rides weren't just about me having fun. Those rides were much-needed exercise for my legs. But I couldn't ask Dad to go through that every

Striking a pose on my Rifton trike

day—not even every other day, not even once a week sometimes. The man was holding down a full-time job, and his weekends were usually pretty full.

There were doctor's appointments for him, Aren, and me.

There were trips to the barbershop.

There were meals to prepare.

There was laundry to do.

When it came to housework, Dad got a little help from his boys. Aren pitched in by vacuuming, doing dishes, packing up laundry, and later putting it away. Aren could also do a bit of cooking, and he was in charge of cleaning up our bedroom. My biggest contribution was reminding Dad and Aren what to do. But I could also clean my plate and dump other garbage in the trash bin. And I could bust a move or two in the kitchen: beating eggs is one of my specialties.

Also on Dad's plate: homework to look over—with SuperMom helping out *a lot* with that via Skype.

Then there was all the stuff my CP demanded of SuperDad. Daily.

Lifting me out of bed and out of my chair to get me toileted and bathed. Seven days a week, week after week after week. At age thirteen I weighed about eighty-five pounds.

Massaging my legs and stretching my arms, sometimes fifteen minutes, sometimes thirty minutes every night before I went to sleep.

Helping me work my door-pulley exerciser to stretch

my arms (five minutes at a time a couple of times a day, every few days).

Added to all that, SuperDad needed to sleep. On weekends when he didn't have a lot of running around to do, Dad was desperate to chill, to just lie on the couch and nap or maybe watch *Animal Planet* or a Korean drama.

Any wonder my Rifton rides became a once-in-a-blue-moon treat?

SOS! Is there a collapsible trike out there for people with special needs? If only I had a magic wand. If I did, before I used it to *zap!* a collapsible trike into reality, I would use that wand to *zap!* elevators for every New York City subway station that needs one. Then people like me could get around so much easier. Faster, too.

After we moved back to the Bronx, I could have gotten to school in about thirty minutes via the 4 train at 170th Street and Jerome Avenue, a few blocks from our apartment. Three stops later we would have been at 149th Street and Grand Concourse, where we could have gone downstairs and transferred to the 2 train.

Five stops later we would have been at 96th Street and Broadway, a few blocks from my school. But . . .

While there was an elevator—a dodgy one—at 96th Street, the 170th Street station had no elevators. Ditto at 149th and Grand Concourse. Because we couldn't take the train to school, Dad was getting up about 4:45 every morning, then getting Aren and me up between 5:15 and 5:30 so we could all be ready for an Access-A-Ride pickup between 6:15 and 6:30. On a good day we got to school by 7:30, when Dad had to clock in.

If it wasn't a good day . . .

If Access-A-Ride was late . . .

If Access-A-Ride had to pick up someone after us . . .

If the Access-A-Ride driver took the long route . . .

If there was crazy traffic . . .

We were late. Late meant Aren and I missed breakfast. Late meant Dad's pay got docked.

Look, I don't know if engineering-wise some New York City subway stations cannot be made fully accessible. But I bet a lot more could be done.

And, no, I'm not beating up on Access-A-Ride. It is

a lifesaver for people who don't have money for cabs.

I really wish more people with full mobility would think about what people like me have to go through to get from point A to point B and join movements for more accessibility in subways and everywhere else. For some, the life they help may be their own.

In the summer of 2013, the Council for Disability Awareness (CDA) reported a scary stat: one in four people, then age twenty, would become disabled before they reached retirement age.

People have workplace accidents.

People get hurt in traffic accidents.

People slip on icy streets.

People slip in bathtubs.

People dive into pools the wrong way.

People fall off balance beams.

I was so surprised to learn that accidents aren't even the major cause of disability. Back problems, heart disease, and other illnesses are. And it's not like you have to have a physical disability to appreciate something like an elevator. I bet thousands of elderly New Yorkers wish more subway stations had elevators to ease their way a bit.

The more I blogged, the more I knew I didn't just want *Aaronverse* to be all about me. I wanted to spotlight other people.

People like an incredible lady I first learned about from a PSA poster in one of my classes: Brooke Ellison. Back in 1990, this New Yorker was hit by a car on her first day of seventh grade. The accident left her paralyzed from the neck down. Even though she was a quadriplegic, Ms. Ellison kept looking up!

Because she kept looking up, she graduated from high school.

Because she kept looking up, she scored 1510 out of 1600 on her SATs.

Because she kept looking up, she got into Harvard University!

In 2000 Ms. Ellison graduated from that great school *magna cum laude*!

Talk about *ability*! Brooke Ellison proves every

bad theory about people with disabilities *wrong*. I really shouldn't call them theories. More like ignorant assumptions. Like thinking that someone with physical challenges also has severe mental challenges. Or like thinking that people with physical challenges actually enjoy being pitied. I'm not saying pity parties don't happen. I'm stressing that generally people with physical disabilities appreciate concrete help and opportunity way more than pity. Concrete help and opportunity like the fabulous Ms. Ellison clearly had.

Terence Moakley was another person I blogged about after I read about him in a newspaper. I had this quadriplegic to thank for things that rarely cross most people's minds, I bet.

Like curb cuts. Back in the 1970s and 1980s, Moakley, president of the United Spinal Association, got some students to identify a bunch of New York City street corners that didn't have curb cuts, which make it so much easier for people in wheelchairs to cross streets. Armed with the data on nonexistent curb cuts,

Mr. Moakley contacted city officials and urged them to construct more of them. Mr. Moakley remained a disability activist for many more years, raising a ruckus, for example, over how difficult it can be for people in wheelchairs to get around the city. Like when they want to or need to use yellow cabs.

Back in 2004, at a crazy-busy taxi stand in Manhattan, Mr. Moakley and several other wheelchair-using people staged a demonstration to show people without disabilities how hard it was for them to get into and out of taxis. That "roll-in" wreaked havoc on street and sidewalk traffic. New York City was embarrassed, but not committed to act on the need for wheelchair-accessible yellow cabs.

Mr. Moakley didn't take no for an answer. Under the banner of Taxis for All, he and other disability activists filed a lawsuit. Change was not swift, but, finally, in September 2014 the Taxi & Limousine Commission settled the lawsuit. At the time only a little over 200 of its roughly 13,000 taxis were wheelchair-accessible. Now it pledged to have 7,000 cabs—about half of its fleet—accessible by 2020. I will be nineteen years old by then and (I hope) in college. Speaking of college . . .

I also used my blog to ask First Lady Michelle Obama to remember the kids with disabilities. This was in response to her initiative to get low-income, minority students to go to college. Worthy cause, no doubt about it—but there was no mention of young people with disabilities.

As part of my virtual protest of this oversight I told my readers about eighteen-year-old Dan, a young man with a disability who dreamed of a career in green energy—but he didn't have a strong support network to help him make his dream a reality. Two years later disaster struck. Dan's dad, his sole caretaker, had a stroke and died. Dan wound up in a group home with all hope of going to college gone. "Poor Dan didn't wish for his fate," I wrote. "His dreams have been crushed into pulp. . . . He had the smarts, but not the supports."

I hadn't read about Dan in a newspaper. I had imagined him. "Guys and gals," I fessed up on my blog, "sorry for this disturbing fictional story, but there's a great possibility that this could actually happen to someone. This could actually happen to me!!!"

Then I addressed the First Lady directly.

> Michelle Obama, if you actually do read this, please take the time to include children with disabilities in your initiative. There are many minority children who are low income, disabled, and are dreaming of a happy future ahead of them. Situations like Dan's actually happen every day.
>
> Michelle Obama, I'd love the chance to meet with you so that you can have a better understanding of what children like me face.
>
> We have bigger dreams than you might expect us to have.
>
> We may surprise you.

I used my blog to spotlight the humiliations people with disabilities experience—and fear. Like wheelchair-using Banetta Grant, a credit-card scammer, who shopped up a storm at Barnes & Noble, Bed Bath & Beyond, Duane Reade, Staples, and a bunch of other stores in Manhattan before she was arrested in October 2013. Later, when Ms. Grant was in a courthouse holding cell waiting to go before a judge, she found herself really, *really* needing to use the bathroom. Her wheelchair couldn't get into any bathroom on the floor where she was held. Had the bathroom and stall doorways been wide enough for her chair, there was another problem: no grab bars to facilitate the shift from wheelchair to toilet.

When Ms. Grant asked a corrections officer to take her to an accessible bathroom in the building—

No.

Result: unable to hold it in, Ms. Grant urinated on herself.

I gathered that when she appeared before the judge Ms. Grant wasn't exactly smelling like roses.

This was me on my blog after I gave people in *Aaronverse* the skinny on what happened to Ms. Grant:

I would like to make something very clear right now.

This goes for everyone no matter what.

NO ONE SHOULD EVER BE DENIED OF USING THE BATHROOM EVER. ESPECIALLY IF YOU ARE DISABLED AND DON'T HAVE THE ABILITY TO GO BY YOURSELF.

This is a violation of human rights, everyone!

It doesn't matter if you've committed crimes or not.

This is unacceptable, everyone.

This should get more attention.

I turned down the volume with this:

No one should ever have their rights stolen away from [them] like this.

NOT EVER.

Ugh, this stuff sickens me.

When I started my blog I didn't know what to expect.

My greeting at the top was "Hi there! I'm Aaron, and I have a disability called cerebral palsy. I'm a disability activist, an artist, alien (yup), and a kawaii person." (For you nonJapanese speakers, *kawaii* is cute or adorable.)

I got even more Japanese in the next lines:

この能力はない障害

("This Ability, Not Disability"—thank you, Google Translate!)

And the next:

instagram: yung.tsukikurisutaru

(young moon star)

What would people think? Yuck, I don't want to follow some disabled dude? Would they think I was creepy? A loser? Wonder what could be cute about somebody with CP? Was I just blabbing into a void?

I was amazed at the people who stepped into my world.

People stepped in with encouragement. I got many, many keep-up-the-good-work comments.

There were great questions, too. One follower asked about my favorite anime TV shows. Answer: *Black Rock Shooter, Beyond the Boundary, Fairy Tail, Bleach,* and *Puella Magi Madoka Magica.* I went on to say that the "battle scenes are just beautiful—they weave so many different types of animation together!"

Sometimes people even asked *me* for advice. Like Anonymous from Maryland who asked how he might help his son draw better.

Answer:

1. Your son can get inspiration from cartoons and anime. If he watches it enough, his drawing will start to get inspired by it. That's what happened to me; maybe it would help you as well!

2. He could try out drawing on the computer with drawing software such as SketchBook Pro 6 or ArtRage. You can find these on Amazon, if you search "drawing softwares." There are tons of expensive ones, but these two are amazing and affordable.

People also stepped into *Aaronverse* with grati-tude: "Hi Aaron!" wrote a young follower. "I just found your blog, and I wanted to tell you how much you inspired me today! I have CP, too; it's great that you're so open about your life with it. I know my mom really wants me to share more with others, but I just have trouble sometimes. Your blog is really encour-aging!"

Most touching of all, people stepped into my world with caring and compassion. After I posted a tribute to SuperMom and SuperDad, someone asked, "How do you cope with not having your mom around?"

I was honest. I replied that it was very stressful. The stress had increased over the years because it had been so long since I had a hug from my mother, a tuck-into-bed from my mother, a kiss from my mother. Not because she had abandoned us or any-thing, but because of drama. Visa drama. Job-loss drama. Other drama-drama. When I started my blog I hadn't seen Mom in four years. Other than via Skype.

* * *

Just as I used *Aaronverse* to tell people about the downs in my life, I also used it to share the ups. Despite my daily challenges and the tough things my family went through, I had quite a few wonderful, surprising, unbe-lievable, game-changing, miraculous, massive, and, yes, *awesome* adventures.

Like the time I starred in a movie.

13
YOU DON'T NEED FEET TO DANCE

OK, "starred" may be a bit of an exaggeration, but I *was* in a movie. And if I hadn't been a student at MSC, it wouldn't have happened, I'm sure.

Back when I was in fifth grade, master djembe drummer Sidiki Conde gave a performance at MSC. Electrifying! What's more, Mr. Conde gave us a bit of a tutorial on the art of the drum. Then it got better.

Months later Dad took me to a playdate like no other. It was at the home of my friend Jonah, who lived near MSC. There was him, a couple other kids from my school, and me, and we all got another drumming lesson from the one-and-only Sidiki Conde.

The whole time, cameras were rolling and boom mikes were bobbing around. Indie filmmaker Alan Govenar was making a documentary about the life and times of this master drummer. When the movie came out, I was in it!

Me in a documentary about drummer Sidiki Conde

You should have seen me that night at the Quad Cinema on West 13th Street. When I first saw myself on-screen, I was absolutely, positively terrified. There I was with a drumstick in my right hand beating a drum. There I was with Sidiki commanding me to beat with the drumstick in my left hand too. And when his friend showed the other kids steps to an African dance, there I was, not stepping back and forth, not jumping up and down, but at least I was trying to do the arm moves. Plus, I led the gang in a round of "Aluna Kande," a song Mr. Conde had taught us when he came to MSC. As I watched myself on-screen at the Quad Cinema I went maniac crazy. I was screaming and carrying on—I was in Excitement City!

I'd like to think that if that happened today I'd be more chill. But that evening I couldn't control myself. The thrill of it was incredible. And exhausting. I slept like a log that night.

Being in a film was thrilling enough, but what made it a *super*thrilling experience was that it was a film about an incredible human being. A new hero for me.

Like me, Sidiki Conde was a March baby. Only he

was born decades before me in 1961 in Guinea, West Africa. Life was normal for him until age fourteen when polio struck and young Conde lost the use of his legs. He did not, however, let his spirit get all shriveled up. He exercised like crazy to make his upper body strong-strong. He learned to walk on his hands. He learned to go up and down stairs on his hands. Mr. Conde learned to dance on those hands too!

When Sidiki Conde grew up he took his ability a step further. With some friends he created Message de Espair (The Message of Hope), a musical troupe made up of other people with physical disabilities and musical abilities. The Message of Hope performed all around West Africa. If that weren't enough, Mr. Conde worked for the National Association of the Republic of Guinea for the Handicapped. He also later joined another musical troupe, Les Merveilles de Guinea (The Wonders of Guinea). With this group he composed, he drummed, and, yes, he danced.

After he moved to America in 1998, Mr. Conde founded Tokounou All-Abilities Dance and Music

Ensemble. That group would perform for and teach people of all ages and abilities at universities, in hospitals, and at schools. Like MSC.

And by the way: the name of Mr. Govenar's film about Sidiki Conde (featuring yours truly) is *You Don't Need Feet to Dance.*

Amen!

Amen!

Amen!

The fact that Mr. Conde became such a wonder, the fact that he didn't let what he couldn't do stop him from developing his talents—that was some rich chicken soup for my soul. I hardly ever saw anybody in a wheelchair really in the swing of things. I hardly ever saw people with disabilities in a movie or on TV (as opposed to able-bodied actors playing disabled people). I hardly ever saw anyone like me working in banks, in schools, as managers of supermarkets or other kinds of stores. I worried that when I grew up I'd be an invisible man. Sidiki Conde's visibility with his disability gave me a whole lot of hope. That's why meeting him at such a young age was HUGE for me. That's why drumming and singing with him again in fifth grade and being in a documentary about him was an absolute BLAST!

I was poised for another blast of a time in sixth grade.

Frost Valley!

14
THIS KID CAN FLY

Sixth graders at MSC get a three-day trip to Frost Valley (FV), a YMCA camp in Upstate New York, in the Catskills. When I went in February 2013, I was a little bummed out at first.

We had been asked in advance to give our top picks for cabinmates. When teachers told us we might not get everyone on our wish list, I thought, fair enough. The way things turned out didn't seem fair at all, though. I got *no one* on my wish list. Instead I bunked with another boy who had CP.

That hurt. I had nothing against my roommate—he

was, in fact, a friend. What hurt was the fact that it was thought that my picks—all kids without disabilities—would be uncomfortable rooming with me because they would have to see my para taking care of me. As I wrote on my blog, "The kids that I picked are very comfortable with my paraprofessional. And, for crying out loud, the kids aren't stupid. OF COURSE THEY KNOW THAT SOMEONE HAS TO TAKE CARE OF ME!" I had asked one or two of the kids on my list if they were up for bunking with me and they had said *yes*! But it was not to be.

As they say, you can't keep a good man down. After my initial disappointment, I was determined to make the most of the trip and have an awesome time.

There was outdoor fun like sledding and skiing. There was indoor fun like gym activities, card games, wood shop, shirt painting, and puzzles.

Had there not been all these activities, FV still would have been a super getaway.

From crowded streets.

From rushing feet.

From noise pollution.

From light pollution.

From pollution-pollution.

That clean, crisp air was so good for my lungs. And the snow-covered maples, frozen lakes, frozen rivers, and roaming deer—I had never seen anything like that before. With something like five thousand acres, Frost Valley was such a great break from my day to day. Though I wouldn't cover all that ground, there was something magical about knowing all those acres were there.

And the food was slammin'—from bacon and eggs to pancakes and sausages for breakfast. One of my favorite dinners was BBQ chicken with pineapple. (Chef Petrone had some serious competition.) As much as I loved the food, it was *so* not the best part. For me, the highlight—the magic moment—was when my turn came to get on the Flying Squirrel.

Three or four kids went before me. As I watched them fly up into the air, I thought, no way. I was petrified. After counselors reassured me that everything would be fine and that the Flying Squirrel would be a great experience, I decided to give it a try.

I was still pretty scared when they strapped me into a harness that was clipped to a rope and a pulley system that would allow the other campers to hoist me into the air.

"Oh my God!" I screamed when I was about a foot off the ground. "Oh my God! This is amazing!" I screamed louder as I was lifted five, ten, twenty, thirty-five feet up—almost to the tops of bare trees. For a brief moment in time—"Hey, everybody!" I wanted to shout out, "This kid can fly!" For that minute or so that I was suspended in the sky, I felt like an angel.

During the three-hour bus ride back to New York City and for days later, I had my heart set on going back to FV. With help from some of Aaron's Angels, I did more than just dream about it. Before the month was out, I got in it to win it—a Facebook contest to win a session (a two-week stay) at FV in the summer.

For the contest, I submitted a short video of me

remembering FV, a video that included a cutaway of me on the Flying Squirrel. And (woo-hoo!) I won. And that was a woo-hoo for two: Aren would be coming with me.

The minute I got back home from that three-day trip, I had told Aren all about it. I went on and on for hours until Dad told me to be quiet and laid down the law: nine o'clock, lights out! So, yeah, Aren was definitely psyched about going to FV in the summer.

All winter, all spring, Aren and I so looked forward to cool experiences, to making new friends (who would, of course, also be cool). From July 14 to July 28, 2013, we just knew we would be in paradise. I planned to blog my butt off about it.

"Sorry about being off for a long time," I blogged on day five of my summer session at FV. As I explained to my readers, I was a no-show in *Aaronverse* because I had been sick. Then I caught my readers up on the fab time I had day after day, from sunup to sundown. In between I kept busy with activities in my camp village, while Aren kept busy in his. There was also "Hangout Time," when I often sat around talking with other campers and sometimes had a counselor lay me down on the grass so I could look up at God's Blue Sky Room. At night, I gazed and gazed at the clear sky, at the shining stars. I LOVED Frost Valley!

I loved the birdsong, the deer spotting, and meeting the camp's pet snakes, Sammy and Houdini. I also loved a challenge someone put before me.

That challenge came on day two: Lake Death.

I had learned to swim in the summer of 2011 at the Jewish Community Center (JCC) not far from my school. This was thanks to one of my Angels. She got JCC swimming pro Michael Jacoby to give me free lessons. (And, yes, Mr. Jacoby became an official member of Aaron's Angels.)

Getting into a pool is one thing. Getting into Frost Valley's Lake Cole, which I called "Lake Death"—no, no, no.

Yes, yes, yes, Vlad the Challenger kept saying.

Vladimir Nahitchevansky was my para/counselor.

"Come on, buddy!" he urged. "It'll be fun! Don't be scared. I won't let *anything* happen to you."

"NOOOOOOO! I don't want to go in! I'm terrified!" I said in my best scaredy-cat voice.

"Aaron, can you at least *try* for me? Please?"

Finally I gave in and we headed for Lake Death with Aren by my side. Once there, Vlad lifted me out of my wheelchair and carried me into the water.

"AAAAAAAAAH! It's freezing cold!" Yes, that was me. Soon, though, I was splashing water in Vlad's face, laughing, getting splashed back, and having the best time! Aren looked on, so happy to see me having so much fun.

Later, when we were on the beach drying off, Vlad told me that he was proud of me. I was proud of me too and so grateful to Vlad for creating an opportunity for me to conquer a fear. For the rest of that day, I was a very, very happy camper.

I was an *ecstatic* camper during our overnight camping trip. Best moment: around a monster camp-fire, about twenty kids and I told jokes and acted stupid.

Friendships became even stronger that night. My new friends included supernice Max, superinnovative Hudson, supercool Phoenix, and superfunny Nathan. The whole business of bonding was probably made a little easier because FV is an electronics-free zone. (How did I blog? I was allowed to use one of the computers in the camp's office.)

At first it felt a bit weird to be without my cell phone and my tablet, but after awhile I truly felt liberated and became a fan of FV's "disconnect to reconnect" policy. And around that campfire during our overnight, that's what we did. We connected, we reconnected. We became a community.

Nothing could top that camping trip. But I paid a price. The next day, I was down for the count with fever, congestion, coughing, sneezing—the whole nine yards. I was in bad shape. So bad that Vlad had to feed me.

After three days of sick, I was back in action. Part of that action was throwing down at a talent show at Frost Valley's MAC village. Mainstreaming At Camp (MAC) serves kids with developmental disabilities like autism and Down syndrome. By day MAC village kids mix in with the rest of the campers. But at night they live in their village with lots of specially trained support people. It was on a weekday night that Vlad the Challenger urged me to enter a MAC village talent show.

When my turn came, I wheeled myself onstage and knocked them dead with a story about a gummy bear who saves the world.

One of the best things about Frost Valley was having so many options for activities. While Aren and other

Summer trip at Frost Valley! I am my own canvas. . . .

kids might be doing things I couldn't do—like archery, soccer, basketball, running themselves silly—I might be swimming or playing a card game or doing a puzzle. Or lying on the grass staring at the beautiful blue sky and mesmerizing mountains.

Sometimes I got a kick out of just hanging out around the ga-ga pit or the basketball court. Sometimes I did that hanging out with my brother, which was easy because we were in the same village. Sometimes I did that hanging out with Vlad.

As the folks who hang out in *Aaronverse* learned, I spent a lot of time with Vlad, naturally, as he was my legs and my lifter—and so much else. Vlad didn't just take care of my physical needs, he was really and truly *with* me—getting to know me. We talked a *lot*! About issues of the day, about my issues—feeling lonely at school, feeling underestimated at times, and the weird way people look at me because of my CP. Vlad and I talked about silly stuff too.

* * *

Not every moment at FV was blue skies and stars, though. There were some glitches—like upon my arrival. As I shared in *Aaronverse*:

> I had some hardships there. I'm definitely not blaming anyone, it was just regular. For example, when we first came to FV, the lodge entrance didn't have a ramp. They paged the maintenance crew for a ramp. My counselors and I waited for about 30 minutes. They didn't come yet. Then, we decided to put me into my manual chair. They lifted me and my manual chair up the bump. After that, they LIFTED the mechanical wheelchair up the bump, too. Then, everything was settled. 2 days later, the ramp was there! No more getting lifted up and down the bump. Hooray!

When I look back on that post, "it was just regular"—wow! How I had matured. A younger me might have started freaking out. It's not that such glitches weren't frustrating and, yes, embarrassing, at times, but I was learning to handle these things better. A bit.

As I also told my blog buds, even with all the clear blue sky and the starry nights, even with the wonderful new friends, I missed home. I didn't miss my neighborhood with its loud music (especially in the summertime), with its exhaust fumes and horn honking from so many cars, and with its *screech-rumble-screech* of the 4 train passing by. No, I didn't miss a place. I missed *home*.

I missed my mom and dad. I missed hearing the Skype ringer going off. I missed the kung-fu movies that my dad watched every night. It was very different without them. The cooking there was really good, but I missed my dad's cooking. I missed my dad's laugh.

As my time at FV was coming to an end, I started missing Vlad, especially after he told me he would not be coming back next year. "I'm going to miss him beyond the limits OF MISSING," I wrote on my blog:

My paraprofessional/counselor Vladimir, I don't have words to describe him. He's one of my best friends now. He did an amazing job of working with me. He took care of me, as if I were family. He made sure I was OK every 5 minutes (not annoying at ALL!), showed me most of the stuff in the surroundings, like animals, plants, stuff I wouldn't normally see, A LOT of really cool stuff.

I can't describe how nice he was to me.

When I was sick, he would constantly play music, dance around, basically try everything to cheer me up. I let a weak smile come across my face. Behind that smile was a huge grin. He said that hanging out with me made his day everyday. I remember how every morning, he would greet me with a hug. He would always be by my side, or relatively close to me. . . . He wasn't a paraprofessional. He was a BFF.

Most of the drawings I made at Frost Valley were for Vlad, who gave me his phone number on the last day of camp along with a note. He said I had changed his life. Our parting was heartbreaking. "As we said good-bye, tears were welling up in my eyes," I blogged unashamedly. "I kept them in. 10 minutes after he left, I was in tears. I miss him SO much."

I was also going to seriously miss my other new friends. Real friends—kids who looked out for me, made sure I was OK.

They all were kind, supportive, and they didn't leave me out of *anything*. Despite being in a wheelchair, they made me a part of their families. They welcomed me into their wonderful, wonderful world. And I did the same. Saying good-bye to them was painful too. I burst into tears. But there was one consolation. We vowed to keep in touch by phone, by email, by Skype, and in *Aaronverse*.

Aren and I did return to Frost Valley the next summer. This time for a double-session, but for a reason that was not great at all.

But before that came Tumblr.

Then *Tanda*.

Before all of it, there was the Frederator.

15
THE FREDERATOR

Serendipity. It means a fortunate happening or pleasant surprise. It means the stars aligning in a magical way.

Serendipity was definitely at work when one day, Angel Deb happened to read an article about David Karp and learned that Fred Seibert, a friend of Karp's mom, had mentored him when he was a teen. Mr. Seibert had let young Karp hang out, then intern, at his animation company, Frederator Studios.

Angel Deb knew I was a huge fan of Mr. Seibert's work (with *Adventure Time* at the top of my list). So she wrote to him in early September 2012. Angel Deb told

Mr. Seibert that he was one of my heroes and about my passion for art and animation. She told him that I was an immigrant, about my family's struggles, and about my CP. She also told him that she had seen the following on his website.

Does it seem strange for a former jazz cat to morph into a TV executive, and then turn into a cartoon producer who sets out to pioneer the new frontier of video on the internet? Not to me. For me it's all part of a very clear continuum. I'm attracted to community, to places where disenfranchised people find what they love, and find each other, and get creative. I'm attracted to heart and soul and humor, and to things that are wild, weird, and unpredictable. I guess you could say I'm attracted to crazy. With any luck I'll have a few more crazy lives to add to this document in the years ahead.

Angel Deb then informed Mr. Seibert that I once said of myself, "I'm just crazy and creative!" She then asked the Frederator to please find time in his super-busy schedule to meet with me. Then she waited.

And waited . . .

And . . .

A few days before Superstorm Sandy hit in October 2012, there I was with Dad, Aren, and Angel Deb at Frederator Studios in Manhattan's Flatiron district. Another miracle in Aaronland.

Believe me, I was ready! I had done a ton of research on Mr. Seibert—from his childhood to his days at MTV, Nickelodeon, and Hanna-Barbera; to how he started Frederator Studios. I wasn't shy at all about letting Mr. Seibert know that I knew his history. I *wanted* him to know how much I knew about him. Why?

One thing I've learned from my life with CP is that I have to be ready. I know that throughout my life I am going to need people. So I press and stress to impress—to let people know that I take them seriously—seriously enough to study up on them—in hopes that they will take me seriously too. And help me.

Mr. Seibert did. He looked through a big, thick folder of my drawings. He let me read him my story about a girl who survives a catastrophe on earth and emerges with superpowers (and green hair). I showed him animations I had done using Flipnotes on my Nintendo. As Mr. Seibert wrote on his blog, I was full of questions, from how long it takes to make a cartoon to financing a show.

Right before we left, the great and wonderful Frederator, creator of my favorite cartoon, said to me something he had said to David Karp years ago. "Aaron, you can come visit me as many times as you like, as often as you like, until you're bored!" As I later told the folks who hang out in *Aaronverse*, "I mentally exploded into confetti!"

The Frederator really blew my mind later. He did the most fantastic, magical, out-of-this-world thing for me. (I'm sure with a bit of urging from Angel Deb.) You guessed it: Angel Fred, Tumblr's first investor, nudged David Karp to invite me into his world. That's how I came to meet with Mr. Karp at Tumblr in June 2013. What do I remember about that historic meeting? Zip! Nada! All I remember is being in awe and astonishment. Then when Mr. Karp invited me to come back and speak to his staff—wow!

Me?

Why?

Because I was creative, maybe? And because I represented diversity, something Tumblr is all about.

A few months later, there I was welcoming the folks at Tumblr into my world. The icing on the cake—SuperMom was with us via Skype! Mom was there to see me give my presentation. Mom was there to see me give Mr. Karp a present.

"Our new Tumblr mascot, guys," joked Mr. Karp after he unwrapped it.

It was an anime drawing (signed, of course) of a woman representing diversity.

Then came the adventure of question time!

The people at Tumblr asked about my drawing

process. About my favorite anime series. (*Bleach* was still at the top of my list along with a new fave, *Ground Control to Psychoelectric Girl*.)

When someone asked, "What's your favorite blog?" I stalled for time. "Is it David's blog?" he asked.

Oops! Aaron on the spot! But not lost for words. "You don't post enough," I teased Mr. Karp.

The best question came at the end. Someone asked how the people of Tumblr could help advance the slogan, "This Ability, Not Disability."

Hmmmm.

"You guys are nice to me," I said after a pause. "So you guys can be nice to any person with a disability." I urged them to get to know people with disabilities, then help them!

"That was so awesome." That was Angel David Karp, shaking my hand as his staffers applauded, many rising to their feet. "You feel good?" he asked.

Katy Perry's "Roar" was rising.

Oh, yes, yes, yes! I felt good!

Creative.

Ecstatic.

Shocked.

Lucky.

Proud.

Most of all I felt *validated*.

16
TANDA

"Hello. My name is Aaron Philip and I am the creator of aaronverse.tumblr.com. And I'm the soon-to-be-creator of a book and short film called *Tanda*."

This was from a two-minute and twenty-five second video pitch on Kickstarter. My costar was Angel Dr. Laurie. As she explained to our viewers, she was on the board of ThisAbilityNotDisability.org (TAND. org). This not-for-profit organization was launched in December 2013, two months after my Tumblr talk.

TAND.org's mission in a nutshell is, as its website says, "to continue the work that one 12-year-old boy,

Aaron Philip, started on his Tumblr blog *Aaronverse*."

A bunch of my Angels created TAND.org to promote self-determination, self-advocacy, and all that good stuff in young people like me, and to rally other people around us with loads of support for our dreams so that when we are adults we can have successful lives. Like Dr. Laurie, other Angels saw the real need for outlets and opportunities for kids with disabilities. Remember the fictional Dan I blogged about? That young man who dreamed of a career in green energy but saw his dreams dashed after his father had a stroke and died? He had the smarts but not the support.

Dr. Laurie and others were very well aware that, as she explained to someone, kids like me "often participate in fewer structured youth groups in their communities; these groups typically provide the experiences where children and teens develop leadership and other skills. Schools and community clubs and activities are set up for nondisabled children and youth; those with disabilities may be included, but they may be on the sidelines and not able to fully participate."

To get up and running, TAND.org had heaps of help. There was Max Sebela from Tumblr who helped with the website. Thanks to Angel Deb, chair of TAND.org, there was attorney Larcy Cooper who helped with the process of getting not-for-profit status. After all the i's had been dotted and t's crossed, TAND.org rolled up its sleeves to help me—aspiring writer, cartoonist, and animator—with *Tanda*: the story of a person who gets around on legs in a world where everybody else gets around on wheels.

Artist, advertising ace, and MSC parent Alon Seifert and his crew helped us make the Kickstarter video, shot at CMA.

My Kickstarter launched on January 4, 2014. People could pledge as little as $5 and as much as $1,500. As is the usual, each level had its reward.

Ten people pledged a fiver. (Reward: a huge internet hug from me)

Ten people pledged $40 or more. (Reward: a copy of the book and a free digital download of the movie. Plus, a polar bear hug from me!)

Nineteen people pledged $100 or more. (Reward: two signed copies of the book and an 8x10 print of one of my illustrations)

On and on it went, with four folks pledging $400 or more. (Reward: five signed copies of the book, five different signed 8x10 prints of my illustrations, and a credit as an executive producer of the video!)

To the one Angel who pledged a thousand bucks, I promised everything in the level above, plus a special thank-you video from yours truly.

The goal was $15,000. On February 3, 2014, 209 backers had pledged $16,231.

Amazing!

And what an incredible month it was. Three days after my Kickstarter triumph, the *Today* show aired a segment on me and my Tumblr talk. (Thank you, Natalie Morales!)

Now back to *Tanda*.

It's one thing to have an idea. It's another thing to execute it. "If there's been one thing that I've learned from managing my disability and going to school, it's planning stuff," I told *Aaronverse* followers on the day I posted the fabulicious news that my *Tanda* project had been funded.

Next up for me, I added, was setting deadlines for myself, mapping out story lines, envisioning scenes, coming up with character traits and settings. This stuff was *major* for me. I had always been a good, strong reader, but when it came to writing, I was a mess. I was at no loss for ideas; I came up with some really creative stuff. My downfall? I was very disorganized in my writing. A story line would go off in ten, twenty directions. Characters would be underdeveloped and sometimes plain forgotten. As I explained to folks in *Aaronverse*:

> Children without disabilities learn how to organize themselves by actively participating and listening to the stuff around them.
>
> However, children with disabilities tend to have a really hard time doing these tasks, by getting distracted easily and sometimes, it's just hard.

Simple things like knowing what to do first, second and third when setting up something are easier for typically developing kids to do than kids with physical disabilities, who don't have the ability to move smoothly, get an object, reach for it, grab it and then release it where they want to put it.

For example, some children with disabilities tend to respond to a question or comments slower than normal children do, in some cases.

Because they don't have this experience, their brain's wiring has yet to make those connections, and they don't really know how to yet.

I was one of those children, guys and gals.

It was only after a *lot* of hard work on the part of my teachers and OTs did I show great improvement by sixth grade. On organization. On focus. On meeting deadlines. (I said *improvement*. Not *perfection*.)

Of course, I still needed mucho help with my *Tanda* book and video. Angel Alon helped me noodle the story line a bit. CMA animators Camilo Cárdenas and

Joe Vena, who helped me with the video, also helped me tweak the story. Another CMA staffer, Rachel Rapoport, then director of community programs, arranged for the space I needed to work on it. And, boy, did I work.

I wrote and rewrote. I drew and redrew. I took edits and suggestions. It was a really uplifting experience. I was producing a book and video. Professional artists were taking me seriously. I felt competent. I felt like (yes!) I could continue to dream of a career in the arts.

Tanda is about a guy named, well, Tanda. He works in Toffee Wheel Town as a janitor at a candy factory.

Day in, day out, Tanda lives and works in isolation. The Wheelie people want nothing to do with him. He is CATI. So no one knows about Tanda's One Happy Pursuit (OHP): designing candy. No one knows, that is, until—(scary music, please!)—the day a catastrophe strikes Toffee Wheel Town. It's Tanda to the rescue with one of his candy creations.

Yes, it's a happily-ever-after life for Tanda. Never

will he be CATI again. Plus, he's promoted to candy designer!

In late June 2014, Kickstarter Angels began receiving copies of the book. In early July, the link to the just-under-four-minute video (narrated by yours truly) was sent out (all handled by TAND.org, which had also arranged to get the book printed and bound).

My dream had come true! I was a published author and illustrator! I had a credit as an animator! Not bad for a thirteen-year-old dude.

Today I can really celebrate those achievements and enjoy my memories of the *Tanda* project. Not so in the summer of 2014. That's because when the *Tanda* book and video were released, my family was reeling from yet another crisis.

17
"MY BOYS! MY BOYS!"

Thursday, June 5, 2014, Aren and I had just finished one of Chef Petrone's pastalicious dinners when Dad began complaining of a pain in his stomach.

All right, all right, I was thinking to myself, surely, he'll get better. I was still thinking positively when Dad took a nap. Not a planned nap. He just fell asleep across his bed, something he *never* did. Dad always took his planned naps in the living room on the couch.

Dad later said he hadn't felt 100 percent at work that day, a day when MSC was a student-free zone (Chancellor's Day). Except, that is, for Aren and me. We had to go to work with Dad because there was no one to look after us. Strike that—no one to look after *me*.

On this quiet school day, Dad treated some of his colleagues to a nice breakfast because they really loved it when he cooked. There was some OJ, special bagels, and bacon. The best part was omelets with garlic and onions, green and red peppers, and Chef Petrone's secret seasonings.

Dad felt a weird pain in his chest a couple of times after breakfast. He shrugged it off as nothing. At home that evening, he felt fine and had no problem making dinner. Then came that strange nap.

It was seven-ish when Dad came out of his bedroom. The rest had not helped. Now he complained of a pain in his chest. He drank a little water, then sat down on the couch. The next thing Aren and I knew Dad's face got weird, all contorted.

"Daddy, you're scaring me!" I was trembling.

He was clearly in pain. Still, as planned, when a friend with a package for him hit our buzzer, Dad went downstairs to meet him. No problem.

When Dad came back upstairs—problem.

"Aaron," Dad said, "I don't feel good. I don't know what's happening to me."

Now I was *really* scared.

"I need to get to the hospital." Dad was gasping for air a bit.

Now I was *terrified*. I was terrified as Dad, clearly in agony, insisted on taking me to the bathroom, then getting me into my bed. After that, he told a neighbor that he was going to the hospital and asked her to look in on Aren and me. Leaving our apartment door unlocked, Dad was gone.

8:00 p.m.

9:00 p.m.

10:00 p.m. Still no Dad.

Aren and I were numb, shocked, and not really sure what to do. Panic had a real grip on me. It had me by the throat. I didn't so much fear that Dad would die but that he would no longer be SuperDad. Where would that leave me? It really hit home just how much I depended on him. For so much. Every day.

My brother kept me from losing my mind. His was the cool head. Aren kept saying that Dad had been through a lot already and had survived and so he would get through this too. I remember at one point we were talking about other things, things I can't remember, but things that I know distracted me from my panic, from my worry, from the wait.

11:00 p.m. Still no Dad.

During the wait, our neighbor, Angel Gladys, popped in and out, in and out.

Midnight. Still no Dad.

Finally at about one in the morning, Aren and I went to sleep. And God watched over us. Our apartment door remained unlocked all that night. We could have been robbed blind—or worse.

Aren and I woke up the next morning around ten to the smell of Angel Gladys making breakfast.

But still no Dad.

After much struggle, Aren and Angel Gladys managed to get me out of my bed and into my chair.

11:00 a.m. Still no Dad.

Not at noon.

Not at 1:00 p.m.

Not at 2:00 p.m.

Finally, with 4:00 p.m. looming, I called Dad's cell phone.

He was in Bronx-Lebanon Hospital Center, about a seven-minute walk from our apartment. And, he had had a heart attack. From one moment to the next, I was in tears, struggling to take it all in. *My dad?* Flat on his back? *My dad?*

He sounded so tired, so weak.

My dad?

It just didn't mesh in my mind. It just didn't sound right to me.

I later learned that the night before, on his way to getting a cab, two times he went down, doubled over in pain. The pain was so bad the second time, Dad was really scared. "Lord, help me to get to a hospital," he prayed, then dragged himself to the busy main street, where, thank goodness, there was livery cab.

And now on that Friday afternoon, June 6, 2014, my dad was seven minutes away from me but I couldn't get to him, couldn't be by his side. It was a little past four when I got off the phone with Dad. Immediately I called Mom.

"Mom, Dad left for the hospital last night. He had a heart attack." I then arranged for a three-way Skype session.

Mom was hysterical. "Petrone, are you OK?" Mom started screaming. "Petrone, are you OK?" She was *really* hysterical. "Petrone! Petrone!" Mom couldn't believe this had happened, because Dad was so health conscious.

Her Petrone was still in something like shock. When the doctors told him the night before that he had had a heart attack he couldn't believe it. He had really convinced himself that it was a very bad case of indigestion.

It was during this call that we learned that Dad would need to have surgery. Triple bypass. Now Mom really freaked all the way out.

Aren and I had to be her strength. We told her to calm down. We told her not to worry. "Mom," I finally said, "Dad is going to be all right! If I could kick double hip surgery in the butt Dad is going to do the same to the heart attack!"

At the end of the call, I only disconnected Dad. Mom stayed on watching and listening as Aren and I shifted into serious SOS mode. Fast and furious, we searched our phones for numbers and began calling Angel after Angel.

It was about six in the evening when Angel Deb texted Manuela Zamora. Angel Manuela had known me since kindergarten because her son, Rodrigo, and I were in the same class.

Angel Manuela's first thought was to reach out to my para, to see if he could get to our house ASAP. But that was a no-go. It would violate DOE regulations; a para can have no contact with a student outside of school. So instead Angel Manuela asked her husband, Ignacio, if he could free himself for a couple of hours to help me do things like get to the bathroom. (Angel Gladys really couldn't lift me.)

Meanwhile Dad was in his own world of worry. Not about himself but about Aren and me. "My boys! My boys!" he said he kept moaning. He knew there was only so much that Angel Gladys could do. Even with all the meds Dad was on—painkillers, sleep aids, blood thinners, and more—he got himself up, dressed, and ready to check himself out.

"But sir, you have to have surgery," a doctor said.

"I know I have to have surgery," Dad replied, "but the surgery is going to have to wait, OK? I have to see about my sons."

"Sir, are you serious?"

"Yeah, I'm serious. I have to put my kids first."

Just in the nick of time: "Petrone, everything is under control." That was Angel Penny Dow on the phone. "Stay in the hospital."

As it turned out, Angel Manuela's husband didn't have to come up to our place after all. Mom had been in touch with her brother, Anderson, and asked him to get to our place ASAP. Uncle Anderson, who lived in Harlem, reached us by about seven. Finally, someone strong enough to lift me out of my chair! Uncle Anderson also got me washed up and dressed. With Angel Gladys's help, Aren and I already had our bags packed. By about eight, we were ready to decamp. Aaron's Angels had a plan in place. As I told folks in *Aaronverse*, tsunamis of support rained down on the Philip boys.

By eight thirty that night, Aren and I were in an apartment not far from our school, in the Zamoras' lovely, loving home, where Angel Ignacio would do the heavy lifting (of me) and where Aren and I would sleep on a daybed that converted into a king-size bed. But yikes! The Zamoras had a schnauzer! And I was *terrified* of dogs. I guess you could say I made lemonade out of that situation. After about a week with the Zamoras, my dog phobia was history.

My fears started to recede on the night we arrived, when we went out with the family to walk their dog, Thunder, and to take in a beautiful night. As Angel Manuela later said, "Some type of de-stress was necessary!" For sure. All the while that I was in SOS mode, I had been in Stress City. In Guilt City too. Not the first time.

No matter how much I knew, believed, understood that Mom and Dad truly loved me, there were times when I couldn't help but feel like a horrible burden, a serious liability because of my disability. My parents had long ago lost an amazing life together in Antigua and so much else. Now Dad, who had the task of lifting me several times a day, had had a super-max heart attack.

Looking back on those two harrowing June days, I think the crisis was hardest on Mom. She knew in her bones that stress had caused Dad's heart attack. She believed it even more after she learned that the doctors had found no calcium deposits, no fat in Dad's arteries. What else could it be but stress? Dad agreed.

Dad had traded places with Mom in 2004. It had been ten long years of stress after stress after stress— the loneliness, the joblessness, dealing with social services, dealing with insurance companies, dealing with my surgeries, dealing with homelessness. And there was the everyday work of ME.

Mom was seriously stressed out too. It had been five years since she had seen Dad and me in the flesh. Two years since she had seen Aren in the flesh. Skype was a blessing, but not enough. As they say, ain't nothing like the real thing.

Back when Dad could afford for us to visit Antigua for the summer, when the time came for us to return to the States, it was so heartrending for Mom. When our trips stopped after money got so tight, she endured indescribable heartache, sorrow, depression. There were crying jags. There were times when she woke up in the middle of the night, fearful and with her heart racing. Then she sent Aren to America. She was so alone.

Two nights after the Zamoras took us in, Mom landed in the hospital.

Panic attack.

18
TSUNAMIS OF SUPPORT

Some time during our first night with the Zamoras, another Angel, very experienced with caring for kids with special needs, texted Angel Manuela asking how she could help. Manuela took her up on her offer.

That Angel was at the Zamoras' early the next day to show Angel Manuela how to move me from the bed to my chair. After other necessaries were done thanks to Angel Ignacio, there was breakfast, then we were off to school. Yes, on a Saturday. It was the annual MSC Uptown County Fair day, a fund raiser.

When Aren and I got to MSC, I had a feeling

everybody knew about Dad's heart attack. People went out of their way to keep Aren and me mad-busy, and I was all for that. Along with getting my face painted, I ate a lot for no good reason. I was desperately trying to do anything to get my mind off my dad. I felt very alone, sad, empty. Every year Dad was with us at the fair. His absence felt awful.

I remember a PTA mom who started crying, then came over to give me a hug. I remember friends struggling to comfort me, as they didn't know what it was like to have a father—and someone you depended on for just about everything—about to go through heart surgery. Of course, it wasn't their fault. They had never rolled a block in my wheelchair. Still it was painful that my friends couldn't comfort me when I needed them the most. Instead I wound up putting my all into trying to keep *them* happy.

Finally Monday arrived, the day of Dad's surgery. Though I was still quite worried about my dad, and once or twice I wondered if he would make it, I actually think that was one of our strongest days. For the most part, Aren and I kept our heads up and our spirits high.

Aren and I were in school when Dad went under the knife at Montefiore Hospital, at about ten in the morning. The surgery lasted four long hours. I don't remember much about what was said when Aren and I spoke to Dad later that day. All I remember about that conversation was me asking him, "Are you safe? Are you happy?"

I also don't remember anything about our conversation with Mom that day. I don't think she was exactly happy, but she was okay. After checking her blood pressure and other vitals, the doctors at the hospital in Antigua had let her go home the night before.

The day after Dad's surgery should have been an insanely happy day for me because that evening I had a solo art show in CMA's Pepperman Family Fine Arts Studio. CMA had exhibited children's art before, but I was the first young person to have a solo show.

There was food and drink and a very nice turnout. More than a few Aaron's Angels were in the crowd, including Dr. Laurie, Penny Dow (but not her daughter, my friend Cookie, because she had soccer practice), and my FV para/counselor, Vlad, who brought along his sister, Nina. My brother and my MSC bud Sam were the only kids. The fact that I had only two peers at the exhibit (and one was my brother) was a stark reminder that, yep, outside of school, I spent most of my time with adults.

Definitely for me, with my CP, had it not been for so many adults befriending me, I never would have had so many magic moments: from meeting Fred Seibert and David Karp, to giving talks at Mercy College and doing the *Tanda* project.

And there was information technology exec Barrett Touhy, who started out as a friend of an Angel and wound up an Aaron Angel, himself. Back in July 2012, after he heard that our apartment was sweltering, he visited to see for himself that our place was indeed Volcano House! It wasn't just a matter of discomfort for me. Because of my CP, I can't afford to sweat too much or I could have a heat seizure. Mr. Touhy went into his own pocket to buy us an air conditioner. And some furniture. And some kitchenware. Touhy's concern about me and my disability wasn't a one-off. He later became vice chair of TAND.org.

And there was *New York Times* columnist Jim Dwyer. He visited MSC in late October 2011. He was one of several amazing people I got to meet thanks to the "Meet a Professional" program Angels Deb and Mary created. It was one of the many ways they told us kids with physical challenges that we could fly. On a "Meet a Professional" day, we got to ask men and women of achievement all kinds of questions.

What impact did their education have on them?

What did they like about their school days?

What did they hate about their school days?

What challenges did they face in school?

When did they know they wanted to be an actor or a doctor or a scientist or a journalist?

When Jim Dwyer met with me and a couple of other kids with physical disabilities, before he addressed our entire fifth-grade class, he read some of our writing and gave us heaps of encouragement. Then he became an Angel. Angel Jim also did really, really help-ful things like put Dad in touch with Jack Doyle of New Settlement Apartments. It was Angel Jack who helped us get out of Hale House and into an apartment.

Speaking of Angels: had CMA never started that Inclusive Arts program, I never would have had my solo art show there on June 10, 2014.

Barbara Hunt McLanahan, CMA's executive direc-tor, Jil Weinstock, curator and director of fine arts, and another staffer Rachel Rapoport were the driving force behind my work being in that art exhibit. Aware of my family's new crisis, they also put together a silent auc-tion overnight. Much to my surprise, of my fourteen pieces on exhibit, nine were sold. One of the ones that sold was *Supersprinkles*, a floating superhero ice-cream cone. Another was *Happy*, an anime face with rainbow tears.

The money I earned from my art was definitely needed, and having the show in the first place was like a miracle, but . . .

If only Dad could have been there. He had *so* been

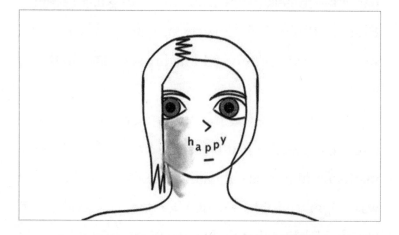

looking forward to it. Just like at the school fair, his absence felt awful. That's why I wasn't happy to the max that evening. Instead, I was like my artwork *Happy*. I had rainbow tears inside.

When the CMA exhibit was over, so was our time

with the Zamoras. Next stop—the home of Penny Dow, who also lived near my school.

Dad got out of the hospital a few days after my CMA show, on one of our family's most important dates: June 13, Aren's birthday. Some of our Angels saw to it that Dad's discharge didn't overshadow it. A few MSC parents—Angels Penny Dow, Tamar Segal, and Nancy Easton—threw Aren a party in our apartment. That was on a Friday. Aren and I hadn't seen Dad in over a week.

He was covered in the sticky marks left by adhesive bandages. He had bruises, scratches, and needle marks on him. Dad's then-unhealed scar on his chest was slightly visible, enough for me to make it out. Seeing him like that had me in Worryville quite a bit. Aren's birthday party, which started at about five, was a much-needed distraction, a really great cheer-up for us all. It was a cozy party with a loving feeling in the air, especially with Mom there via Skype. Two kids were also at the party: my friend Cookie, and Sadie (Angel

Nancy's daughter), who was in Aren's grade.

It was fun while it lasted, which wasn't all that long. When the party was over, it was back to the Dows for Aren and me, since Dad wasn't well enough to take care of us yet.

I wish it had been smooth sailing from then on, but Dad had some complications and wound up in the hospital soon after! When would Dad catch a break? We had so much help from so many Angels during that time: Aunt Shirley's mother, Aunt Cathy, came down from Boston to stay with Dad for a week. After the Dows, Aren and I stayed with Karin Spraggs, mother of my classmate Oli, who is also in a wheelchair. I gotta believe that our time there was less stressful for them than it was for the Zamoras or the Dows because Angel Karin had so many years of experience taking care of a kid in a wheelchair. Plus, Oli's father, Arthur, came by a couple of times to help, and Oli's brother, Malcolm, was on hand to help out, too. A lot.

After several days with the Spraggs, our next stop—

Home.

For good.

And with big help.

A band of MSC parents—Manuela Zamora, Penny Dow, Tamar Segal, Abbie and Lewis Wendell, Kim Atkins, Sidsel Robards—held an online fund raiser for us through Crowdrise. They raised enough money for one home aide to take care of me by day—including getting Aren and me to and from school—and another aide to take care of me at night. (Dad could do no heavy lifting for a long while.) We had that round-the-clock help until July 14, the day Aren and I left for Frost Valley. Instead of one two-week session we would be there for two sessions, from July 14 to August 8. Another gift from Aaron's Angels, who really understood how much Dad needed peace, quiet, no worries, and lots of rest.

After we left, Dad continued to have a tsunami of support. There were groceries delivered to his door. One MSC parent had seven-grain bread and five-bean soup delivered. Dad was overwhelmed by all the generosity. So was I, though I knew it couldn't, wouldn't last forever, that it would slowly fade away.

It was hard for me to understand that tsunamis of support can't last forever because people have their lives to live, their own crises and problems to deal with.

Anyway, while Dad was enjoying bread and soup, I was having a very interesting, very different time at Frost Valley.

19
ARENVERSE

When I got to camp, there was a challenge right off the bat. It was a much bigger deal than the entrance of a lodge lacking a ramp.

I wouldn't be staying in the village for thirteen-year-old girls and boys as expected, because that village wasn't wheelchair accessible. I was given a choice: join a village for kids younger than me or the one for fifteen-year-old boys and girls.

Immediately, I was in Panicville! As scared and nervous as I was, I was also a little thrilled. Here I was faced with making a decision. Here I was put in a position of being independent, which wasn't something that happened to me very often. After a good fifteen minutes of mental lollygagging I decided to take my chances with the older kids.

As I rolled up the hill to Quirk Lodge, where I'd be staying for four weeks, my stomach churned and I was sweating heaps. It wasn't just the heat. It was fear. I was regretting my decision already but I was at a point of no return: My wheelchair was almost out of juice; I needed to recharge my battery.

They're teenagers!

Are they mean?

Nice?

Will I be able to open up to them?

I was in a tsunami of negativity when I reached Quirk Lodge. I was really scared of teenagers at the time. But I couldn't turn back.

Frost Valley was still a magical place, so I got recharged too. I really took it easy. I was a lot more subdued. Some of the things that interested me before no longer did.

Like swimming. Most of all I had lost interest in going out of my way to make friends. I had spent most of my life engaging people, trying to dazzle them even. With kids my age, I had so often tried to get them to be my friends with my wild-and-crazy, superfriendly act. In the summer of 2014, that Aaron was fading away.

Months earlier I'd written about my friendship angst in a poem I titled—what else?—"Friends."

> *Distant, yet close*
> *Jealousy, yet gladness*
> *Happiness, yet sadness*
> *Deception, yet happiness*
> *Greed, yet sorrows*
> *Secrecy, yet love*
> *Love, yet hate*
> *Fake smile, yet almost no one knows*
> *Betrayal, yet retribution*
> *Bias, yet your own self-exception*
> *You never actually know who your friends are.*

I don't remember what inspired that poem. Something somebody did to me? Said to me? Whatever it was, it clearly had me feeling lonely and low. Angry, too.

For those first few days at camp I was pretty much in Lonerville. Most of the teenagers in my village said little more than "Hi" to me. Things began to change after a few days. The turning point was Devo.

Devo, short for Devotion, is a time when members of a village meet up to play games, do activities, and talk about their lives. When my turn to talk came, I told everyone about my dad's heart attack and how hard it is to be a thirteen-year-old in a wheelchair. I was overwhelmed by the response. I was no longer in Lonerville! The same thing happened in session two when a new bunch of teens entered our village. I started out in Lonerville but after a soul-to-soul time known as Vespers, when I spoke from my heart about all the challenges, frustrations, and worries that stem from my CP, so many of those fifteen-year-olds became really nice to me, showed me so much love. They told me how strong I was. They told me they thought that I was amazing.

Meanwhile Aren had been having a ball. With us being in different villages, my brother and I only saw each other for brief periods of time every few days. But I knew he was enjoying himself. I could see it on his face during our meet-ups. (Plus, I had my sources).

When it was time for us to leave Frost Valley, both Philip boys were feeling on top of the world.

Back from Frost Valley soon meant back-to-school time, back to our regular routine.

"Aaron and Aren, it's time to get up!" Dad shouts. It's about five thirty as I roll over onto my back and wait for him to pick me up and carry me to the toilet. My brother is still sound asleep under his thick blanket on the top bunk. I envy him—Aren almost always gets an extra fifteen minutes of sleep.

After my dad cleans me up, he gets me dressed, and I brush my teeth. I have trouble doing my hair due to limited mobility, so I rely on Aren or my dad to pick out my really tightly curled hair. It. Hurts. So. Much. (First choice Dad. Aren can be like Attila the Hun with an Afro pick.)

There was a time when I really lamented the fact that someone has to help me go to the bathroom. It was the biggest reminder of my lack of independence. In time I got more relaxed about people-not-my-Dad taking me to the toilet, though I've never had anyone make it as comfortable for me as he does. I've had paras who weren't very gentle, but they've never had to take me to the bathroom all that much. The older I got, the more I trained myself to limit my intake of liquids. There's barely any time in school to go to the bathroom without missing out on something extremely important in class.

Clothes—that's where Dad and I have a problem. I consider myself extremely fashionable but my dad is always picking out the UGLIEST outfits. Every morning we fight about what I should wear. Like the time he paired my really cool black Nike sweater with yellow sweatpants—EW!—and I made him change it to gray sweatpants because I didn't want to look like a bruised banana. We would continue to fight over what I wear because I'd recently decided that I should look as creative, eccentric, and as cool as my art. Basically, that I AM art! Anyway . . .

After all the basics are taken care of, it's time to gear up (our tablets, my headphones, the phone Aren and I share, my laptop and charger, and everything else we need for the day). Aren does the gearing up. I am Mr. Reminder, or at least I try to be. Most of the time I fail, forgetting to remind Dad to grab his phone or my brother to grab his earphones, because I'm not a morning person and I'm not as kawaii as I normally am—not when I have to get up before six.

After I've done all the reminding I can manage, we head outside to meet Access-A-Ride so we can make it to school. If we get there with time to spare, we might hit the Dunkin' Donuts that's two minutes from my school to get Wi-Fi. Wi-Fi is essential to me, I need it to survive. That's how I stay in contact with my internet friends. Because of my limited access to friends in real life, the internet is my safe haven and the one big place I get to be social with kids I met at camp or through my blog—and my good friend Leanna who used to go to MSC. So in the mornings, yeah, I want to check in with my friends. Or I may want to post some art on Instagram, see if anyone new is following me or how many likes I got on something.

Because Dad has to be at work at seven thirty, Aren and I have more time to kill until our school day begins

Me and a friend being kawaii after school

at eight. So we sit in the cafeteria arguing, laughing, eating breakfast. Sometimes Aren plays a game on my computer. (He's obsessed with *Happy Wheels*, a very violent physics game.) Sometimes Aren just has to chill because I need the computer to catch up on some work I missed. Once that half hour is up, Aren and I go our separate ways. This is our typical school morning.

On the weekends and during school breaks, I wake up quite kawaii. That's because I usually don't get up until eleven. Unless there's a doctor's appointment or something, weekends are pretty relaxed and easy for me. All Aren and I do usually is talk to Mom on Skype, laugh, and argue about what we'll watch on TV or about how lazy and annoying we are to each other.

Sometimes I fly solo, talking to my internet friends on Instagram, Kik, and Snapchat about music and art, or posting edits or new artwork on Instagram to show my friends. Sometimes I rant about what it's like to be in a wheelchair to give my followers more insight into Aaronland.

Brand-new piece I'm really proud of, inspired by an awesome shirt I saw!

Weekends and holidays I'm not a total slacker, though. Sometimes I help my dad make lunch. Chef Aaron really excels at peeling vegetables.

And, oh yeah, when there's no school I binge watch *Sailor Moon*, *Tokyo Ghoul*, *Chobits*, *Naruto*, plus a million other animes. The next thing I know, my little brother is slandering me, calling me a "Weeaboo"!

I am not a Weeaboo! My brother is misinformed. Check this definition of Weeaboo from Urban Dictionary: "Someone who is obsessed with Japan/Japanese Culture/Anime, etc. and attempts to act as if they were Japanese, even though they're far from it.

They use Japanese words but usually end up pronouncing them wrong and sounding like total [bleep]."

Does that sound like me? All right, I've had my hair dyed purple and orange or blond so I could have anime hair (sort of). True, I will eat sushi any chance I get, but it's not like I have a closet full of kimonos, hakamas, and tabi socks. And I have it on good authority (myself) that I pronounce words like *kawaii* correctly and do not sound like a total [bleep].

Our Weeaboo wars sometimes last deep into the night. On weekends we normally conk out about one in the morning.

Such was my life in the fall of 2014. Sort of. It wasn't all school-day routine followed by R&R on weekends.

I spent a lot of time with a lot on my mind, worrying.

About Dad mostly. Oh, he was back in action all right, back to being Chef Petrone, back to going above and beyond for his boys, back to heavy lifting. But I wondered, How long can he keep this up? I prayed for his heart to hold out until some help kicked in.

I was supposed to get a new wheelchair in 2015. The

chair I got in 2010 was in bad shape. A while back, the motor had conked out—and we would have been in a real pickle had Angel Fred not paid for the repair. That was a big blessing but not the end of the problem. By 2014 I had outgrown that chair but Medicare will only replace a wheelchair every five years. The fact that I had outgrown my chair meant some pain for me and another task for Dad. Whenever I was stationary, every now and then Dad had to stop whatever he was doing, stand behind me, grab me by my armpits, then hoist me up into a proper sitting position. If not, I'd be sitting on my tailbone for a *long* time. And that hurt! (I had also outgrown my backup manual chair, but we still held on to it because in a power outage, any chair is better than none.)

Along with my chair problem, my leg braces had gone whack on me back in the fall of 2013. Big problemo. I cannot stand or bear weight without them. Not being able to do a little standing caused my legs to become even weaker and my feet to turn sideways. My stander at home wasn't any help either. It was busted.

There would be no new equipment for me until an insurance issue got worked out. Dad got the paperwork done as fast as he could and got the all clear in January 2015. We hoped that by June 2015, I'd have a new chair, new leg braces, a new stander, and a few other things I really needed.

We were also hoping that in 2015 there'd be a home aide to help take care of me a couple of hours a day. What a relief for Dad. Less heavy lifting to do. More time to chill. Until Dad had heart surgery, we weren't eligible for help at home.

In the meantime, while all that good stuff was on the horizon, in the fall of 2014 I had the pressing matter of the high school search.

In NYC, you have a choice of high schools, which is good and bad. Good, because you can pick a big school or a small one; one with lots of arts or one that focuses on engineering, science, the humanities. Bad, because there are tests, auditions, interviews . . . eek! Every eighth grader dreads this process, but here again, I had added challenges to face. I had to eliminate some schools I was interested in after I discovered that there were accessibility issues. Like it might be easy for me to wheel *into* the school, but there was no elevator and so no way for me to get up and down *in* the school. Or there *was* an elevator, but it was too narrow for my chair. In the end I had about a half dozen schools on my wish list. I researched them and prepared as hard as I could for the interviews. Then, like thousands of other kids, I applied and waited to learn in the spring which of the schools that I wanted, wanted me.

Picture from my life, created for my LaGuardia High School audition

I was really nervous about high school. About fitting in. About doing well. Mostly about doing well because I want to get into a good college. And I want to go to a really good college because I want to make something of myself.

I want to thrive in my future.

I want independence in my future, including financial independence.

And I definitely want to give back in my future—like maybe buy a top-of-the-line wheelchair for a kid who has outgrown his. Most of all, I want to give back to Mom and Dad—treat them to the vacation getaways they deserve.

I hope for college even though I have big worries about it. As I told the people at Tumblr, one of my biggest worries is not *not* getting into a college, but physically navigating college and managing my classes. Through my senior year in high school I'll have a para during the school day to take me to the bathroom, to take notes, to hand me things. But after that? In college, Medicaid will only pay for a para for two or three hours a day.

What if I have classes in the morning and in the afternoon?

Would I have to choose classes based on their times of day?

Would I have to cram classes, lunch, and bathroom breaks into the few hours I had a para?

Would I have to, like, do a minifast so I wouldn't need to use the bathroom after the para's time with me was up?

Would I have to wear a diaper to go to college?

Would I wind up a urine bomb?

Would I never be able to go out at night with friends?

In my dorm, what would . . .

I often got really worked up about this, then had to calm way down, reminding myself, first things first. First I had to get through high school. That would mean more and harder academic work. That would mean being with full-on teenagers. That would mean *me* being a full-on teenager. Going to high school would also mean leaving behind my best friend: my little brother, the Laugh Master of my life, who always knows what wacky thing to say or do to make me laugh or smile for real.

School without Aren? You'll handle it, I told myself over and over again, just like I've handled everything else in this crazy life of mine.

20
TRIUMPH (ROAR! PART 2)

The high school acceptance letter arrived on Saturday, March 7—just under a week before my fourteenth birthday.

The wait that day was like no other! We were long gone and up at Mercy College when the mail was delivered. We didn't get back home till around five. (Grrrr!)

I was going bonkers when Dad opened the mailbox—and yes, the letter had come!

I was bonkier still when we got into the elevator and Dad opened it as we made our way up to the sixth floor.

I was crazy anxious as I listened to the words forming

in my dad's mouth. He said that I wasn't accepted to LaGuardia High School, but instead I got into NYC Lab School for Collaborative Studies. At first I was really sad about LaGuardia kicking me to the curb. I had *so* wanted to be a part of that diverse, artsy community since *fifth grade*!

I was in a wicked funk until I thought about all the positives of Lab. It is extremely close to Frederator and Tumblr, so it would be a million times easier to go there. I already had one of my very best friends at Lab, Dani, an MSC alum. Dani had vowed that if I got into Lab, she'd see to it that I had the best time ever. Then I thought about all the great food places near the school, in the really cool neighborhood of Chelsea. It took a while but things were soon good again in Aaronland.

Lab, here I come!

And I had finished working on this book with Tonya. What a year!

Writing this book has made me look back on my life and think—wow. My family and I have had so many challenges, so much to overcome—and there's more still to deal with.

But I have to say, I'm also really happy to look back on all the amazing things I've been able to achieve. And it makes me think more about what I hope my story can do once it's out in the world.

I hope it makes folks more aware of the millions and millions of people with disabilities all around them, and help fight the good fight for their rights and greater accessibility.

I hope it makes all my readers realize that *so* much is possible no matter what the difficulties.

I also hope that you'll invite folks of *all* kinds of abilities into your life, now that you've had a chance to hang out in Aaronland.

ACKNOWLEDGMENTS

I would like to give a sincere, heartfelt thank-you to my coauthor, Tonya-senpai (*senpai* is used to describe someone who you look up to in Japanese), for helping me get this book done, putting it in the right direction, and for not getting mad at me despite my gross laziness at times.

I would also like to thank:

My wonderful literary agent, Jennifer Lyons, for being such a cool, calm, and collected person throughout this entire process.

Donna Bray; her assistant, Viana Siniscalchi;

and all of Balzer + Bray, for being such nice, caring people, for putting so much dedication and effort into what they do, and for giving me the opportunity to write this book about my crazy, hectic, wonderful adventure of a life.

All of Frost Valley YMCA, for making me so incredibly happy, especially PAC/Windsong 2014, for being some of the most kindhearted, truthful, and loving people I've ever met; and Vladimir Nahitchevansky, for being one of my best friends until the very end.

The internet, for being there for me when no one was. I know I sound lame but I'm just stating the truth. The internet has provided me with creativity, laughter, bonds, friendships, and everything in between.

My in-real-life friends Reuben, Sam, and Jonah, for reassuring me that I have two lives and that I'm kawaii enough to have them in my life.

Taylor and Nick, for being the sweetest and most supportive internet friends I've ever had.

My best friend Leeann, for making me happy and

inspiring me to think outside the box and be creative on a day-to-day basis. Also, for being the yin to my yang.

My best friend Lara, for being a comfort to me when no one was there, for giving me laughs, for scolding me when I do something incredibly dumb, and for being such a genuine, warm, sweet person.

My occupational therapist Deb, for believing in me, helping me feel as comfortable as I can in school, pushing me to think as hard as I can, and for being such a role model and inspiration in life.

My occupational therapist Mary, for keeping me on track 24/7, for helping me expand my knowledge, use logic, and for being such a lovely person overall.

Dr. Laurie Olson, for helping my family and me out during tough times, for making me smile, and for radiating so much love and positive energy.

Last, I would like to thank my mom, dad, and little brother, Aren, for giving me never-ending love and support throughout my life, art, and activism. You have helped me blossom into the person I am today, and I really love you guys.

Thank you all so much.

So much love to all of you.

—A.P.